Stealing the Wild

Stealing the Wild

BETH HODDER

Stealing the Wild
by Beth Hodder
Copyright ©2010

 Published by Grizzly Ridge Publishing, P.O. Box 268, West Glacier, MT 59936.

10 9 8 7 6 5 4 3 2 1

ISBN 978-0-9793963-1-1

Printed in the United States of America

Library of Congress Control Number: 2010905392

Attention schools, colleges and universities, corporations, and writing and publishing organizations: Quantity discounts are available on bulk purchases of this book for educational training purposes, fund-raising, or gift giving. For information contact Marketing Department, Grizzly Ridge Publishing, P.O. Box 268, West Glacier, MT 59926

Cover Illustration by Guy Zoellner
Map of Schafer Meadows by Guy Zoellner
Interior Design and Typesetting by Donna Collingwood
Manuscript Editing by Florence Ore

For more information: www.grizzlyridgepublishing.com

This is a work of fiction. Names and characters in this novel are the product of the author's imagination, or, if real, are used fictitiously without any intent to describe their actual conduct. Institutions and places in this novel are real. However, the political and administrative settings of this novel are not meant to represent the actual policies of any institution or law enforcement agency.

In celebration of the life of Marian Jean Hodder Strange
My beautiful sister

Acknowledgements

I received generous help from many individuals in writing this book. I wish to thank Reba Spain, Joanna Spain, and Shana Lara for reading and critiquing the manuscript. Their discerning advice and ideas helped me achieve a comfort level I needed.

Thad Wollan read the manuscript with a teacher's eye while I struggled with the appropriateness of this difficult topic for young readers.

Game Warden Perry Brown, Montana Department of Fish, Wildlife and Parks, helped me understand a game warden's job in hunting and capturing poachers. He also provided valuable insights that led to a much needed change to the book's ending.

Conservation Manager Keith Roberts, Friedkin Conservation Fund, Arusha, Tanzania, spent time with me over Tanzanian coffee and through email discussing the effects of large-scale poaching on the fate of animals in African countries.

Veterinarian Dr. Bill Vance, Fort Collins, Colorado, gave me initial information about poaching and started me off in the right direction.

Law Enforcement Officer Cathy VanCamp, U.S. Forest Service, Gila National Forest, read the manuscript and provided advice about a Forest Service law enforcement officer's role in dealing with poachers.

Retired Spotted Bear District Ranger Dave Owen explained controversies that resulted from the Wilderness Act becoming law.

Capri Little, Snowy Springs Outfitters, gave detailed descriptions of Scott Lake and Flotilla Lake and told stories of poachers and caching in the Great Bear Wilderness.

Children's Librarian Eileen Sullivan, Silver City (New Mexico) Library, researched books for me on poaching written by other authors for children.

Susan Kemper helped me understand fly fishing and the right flies to use in different situations.

Mary McNeill and Maxine Watkinds helped me way more than I can repay, going over the manuscript again and again, finding errors, suggesting changes, and generally offering sage advice.

And thanks to my husband, Al Koss, for information on wilderness, trail maintenance, Leave No Trace, Schafer Meadows, and the bear at Gooseberry Cabin, and for proofreading the manuscript.

Books by Beth Hodder

Jessie and Oriole Mystery Series

The Ghost of Schafer Meadows (2007)

Stealing the Wild (2010)

Praise for
The Ghost of Schafer Meadows

*"***** FIVE STARS! Author Beth Hodder brings her career as a Forest Ranger to vivid and colorful life, teaching about the wilderness through the eyes of a smart girl on the verge of becoming a teenager. Filled with suspense, mystery, a haunting ghost, and a bit of danger, this story is sure to please! *****"*

—Detra Fitch, *Huntress Reviews*

"Author Hodder's first-hand experience and connection with the Montana wilderness is evident as she captures a strong sense of place and takes the reader on a vivid journey. Readers will feel as if they are there, an experience they will want to duplicate in real life."

—Janet Muirhead Hill, *Norris, MT, author of the "Starlight and Miranda" Series and "Danny's Dragon"*

"It's clear [Hodder has] a gift for writing. Clean, short sentences, great description, impeccable grammar, and an intriguing plot made for a fun, swift read...in a long-lost Nancy Drew sort of tradition."

—Judy Rosen, *Estes Park, Colorado*

"I think [Hodder] captured what a 12-year-old girl is really going through, with moving away from friends, being angry with her dad and having crushes on boys and older guys. Plus the imagery of the area makes me feel like I'm in the middle of the forest. I can picture everything in my mind."

—Kelly Earick, *Florence, KY*

"I loved your book!! It had so much detail and excitement that I could not put it down. It is now my favorite book."

—Maggie Balan, *Snohomish, WA*

"I loved your book! I read it through in one sitting because I simply could not put it down...the description makes me feel like I am there with Jessie and Oriole."

—Alexandra Ore, *13, Fort Collins, Colorado*

Table of Contents

Book Characters

Schafer Meadows
Jessie Scott's Family
Jessie, 12
Oriole – Jessie's dog
Jed, 16
Tom – Jessie's dad and the Schafer Meadows ranger
Kate   Jessie's mom

Jessie's Friends
Allie Carter, 12
Will Lightner, 12
Casey – Will's dog and Oriole's friend

Trail Crew
Celie Long Runner – crew leader
Mandy Lake
Cody Gray

Others at Schafer Meadows
Don Lightner – Will's dad and U.S. Forest Service law enforcement officer
Carlos Sanchez – Game warden (Montana Dept. of Fish, Wildlife, and Parks)
Pete Randolph – Assistant ranger to Tom
Charlie Horton – Station guard
Jim Gunderson – Pilot and volunteer

Visitors to Schafer Meadows
Lou Wells (Lost) – Cody Gray's friend
Ben Morris – Lone horseman
Four backpackers:
> Wiley (Coyote)
> Emma
> Tracy
> Steve

COX CR.

GOOSEBERRY

CLACK CR.

MIDDLE FORK OF THE FLATHEAD

DOLLY VARDEN CR.

MORRISON CR.

SCHAFER MEADOWS

SCHAFER CR.

SCOTT LAKE

Schafer Meadows & Area Trails

FLOTILLA LAKE

New Friends

You'd think something as simple as inviting a couple of friends to visit would be no problem, but it doesn't seem to work that way for me. What I hoped would be a fun time with two new friends turned into a nearly disastrous mystery. And while my friends were all excited about the blood and gore, I was afraid they'd have to go home, my biggest fear. I was a wreck.

Here's how it all began.

A few weeks ago after my family moved from New Mexico to Montana, I met Will and Allie, two really cool kids. They've known each other since they were five.

Will's mom died when he was eight. He lives with his dad, Don, and Casey, their trained law enforcement dog. They spend their summers at the Spotted Bear Ranger Station, part of the Flathead National Forest in Montana, where Don works as a law enforcement officer.

Allie's parents are friends with Don. They often go camping at Spotted Bear. I met Will and Allie on one of those camping trips, and although we didn't get to spend much time together then, we hit it off right away.

Maybe that doesn't sound like a big deal, but I live at Schafer Meadows, a U.S. Forest Service ranger station deep in the heart of Montana's Great Bear Wilderness. The only other kid at Schafer is my brother Jed, who's 16 and normally doesn't like hanging around with his kid sister. The wilderness has no roads, just trails and a small grassy airstrip, so people get to Schafer Meadows by horseback, hiking, or plane. We don't see many kids, and there aren't telephones or access to cell phones or the Internet. It's hard for me to meet other 12-year-olds or keep in contact with them when I do.

So when my mom and dad asked me if I wanted Will and Allie to come visit for a couple of weeks, I was psyched!

The day after they arrived, Will and Allie joined me for a summer horseback ride. We were headed to Scott Lake near Schafer Meadows to go fishing. A cloudless sky and a pleasant breeze warmed me. And my dog, Oriole, and her good buddy Casey were getting great exercise running up and down the trail. What could possibly go wrong?

Lost in happy thoughts, I smiled as I looked up the trail at the dogs. Then the smile disappeared. I pulled back on Red's reins and used my hand as a visor to shade the sun. "Hey! What's up with you dogs?"

Oriole stopped and stared up at me. The sun backlit her sleek yellow coat and her black ear, eye, and chest for which she got her name. Casey's black Lab fur glistened. Both dogs held tightly to something that looked like a man's tan leather jacket. They growled playfully in a tug o' war, shaking their heads from side-to-side. Each tried to get the other to let go of their prize. When Casey finally gave in, Oriole dragged the object up the trail, her head high. The thing was large and cumbersome, and she kept tripping on it. When at last she stopped and dropped it, both dogs stood over the trophy, sniffing it intently.

Will slid down from Sky, his black horse with a white star on its forehead. "Someone's not going to be happy when they find their jacket torn to ribbons by you two goons. We'd better see if we can rescue it." Allie and I jumped off our horses to join him. The three of us stared when we reached the dogs. Allie bent over to pick up the jacket but jerked back her hand as if struck by a snake.

"Oh, gross, Jessie! That's not a jacket. What is it?"

She gagged like she might throw up.

I leaned closer. "Looks like a deer hide. Eeewww. And it reeks."

I grabbed a stick and tried to lift it, but it was too heavy. "Poor thing," I said. "Wonder what happened to the rest of it?"

Casey and Oriole wandered farther up the trail and stopped to sniff something else. We tied our horses to trees and walked up to see what they'd found. Allie got there first and looked away, her face white.

"It's a deer's head. Looks like a doe. And I think there's a skeleton farther up the trail."

Will's brown eyes looked beyond to where the bones lay. "It's hard to tell from here but animals may have eaten away the meat. Looks like there's hardly anything left."

The deer's head lay on its side at the edge of the trail. Its forehead leaned against a large rock. I've always thought of deer as gentle creatures, especially the females—the does. It was hard to look into its eye, which stared dully at nothing.

I shuddered with horror. "Hey, you guys, look at this. Somebody cut the head off."

Will checked out the deer's head, then hurried to the skeleton and knelt down. "And no animal gnawed on this. Somebody cut the meat from the bones."

Will searched the ground off the trail about 15 feet. "This is creepy! They sawed off the legs, too."

Four legs with small hooves lay under a bush. Will shook his head. "Whoever killed this deer probably didn't think it would be found. Pretty stupid, though, because it probably smells like a feast to bears or wolves. Something must've dragged it out of the woods and onto the trail."

I hurried back to the deer hide and looked closer. Small bits of meat hung on parts of the hide. Someone had hacked it off the body. "It's not hunting season. This deer was poached."

"What does that mean?" Allie asked. She pushed her

round glasses up on her nose and tightened the clip on her long black hair.

"It means they took this deer illegally. You can't just kill animals anytime or anywhere you want. You gotta have a license. And you can only hunt in special seasons."

Will grinned. "Man! This is cool! We haven't even been here a day and already we've got a mystery to solve. Wouldn't it be great to find the poacher? Forget fishing. Let's call our dads on the Forest Service radio, Jessie. They can meet us here."

As a U.S. Forest Service law enforcement officer, Will's dad works a lot in the Great Bear Wilderness. My dad is the wilderness ranger at the Schafer Meadows Ranger Station, so they sometimes work closely together on law enforcement cases.

"Yeah. You're right, Will. We should call our dads." I ran back to Red and grabbed the Forest Service handheld radio.

"Wait a minute," Allie said. "What about the deer? Shouldn't we move it off the trail? What if someone comes by?"

"No," Will said. "Leave it where it is. It's evidence. We don't want to mess with the crime scene. My dad'll know what to do."

I called my dad on the radio and asked him to get Don. We sat along the trail and waited—and waited and waited. The dogs raced down the trail, chased each other back to us, and raced down the trail again. When we got bored we threw sticks for the dogs. Although my friends were excited, my shoulders drooped. I hoped Will and Allie would be allowed to stay and worried that they wouldn't. Sometimes adults get strange ideas, especially when law enforcement is involved. You just never know what they're thinking.

Lost

Dad smiled at us. "It was right to tell us about the deer. I know it ruined your fishing trip, but we'll make it up to you. How'd you like to go camping and fishing after we investigate the deer? You kids and I will go to Scott Lake for lunch and an overnight camping trip, but Don will have to go back to Schafer and contact Fish and Game."

"But we didn't pack for a camping trip," I said.

"I know. We packed for you. That's why it took us so long. Do you want to go or not?"

"Wow, Dad, you mean it?" I looked at Allie and Will and they both beamed. Oriole and Casey sensed our excitement and started to ki-yi and run around us.

I felt much better. My new friends didn't have to leave.

When we reached the deer, my stomach lurched once more and my heart sank. Why would someone illegally kill this beautiful animal?

Don took many pictures of the head, hide, bones, and discarded legs. He put Casey to work. Casey is a highly trained Forest Service law dog. Don had him search the area, even though he and Oriole had done that earlier. It looked like Casey loved being a law dog, because he quit playing with Oriole and sniffed all over for scents. Oriole seemed to understand he was working and sniffed around, too. The dogs stopped about 30 feet off the trail. There was blood and lots of deer hair on the ground. It was probably where the deer was killed and cut up.

Don bagged everything as evidence. He wrapped it in "manty" packs made from heavy canvas tarps and tied it with thick ropes. He loaded the manties on the back of Babe, his big brown mule. Babe had large ears that stuck out to the side and flopped up and down when she walked. She made me laugh when I watched her go down the trail.

"Doesn't Babe mind you putting dead things on her back?" Allie asked. "I'd think the smell would bother her."

Don patted Babe on the nose, grabbed her lead rope and swung into his saddle. He lightly kicked his tan and white horse, Tigger, into a slow walk. Babe walked easily behind Tigger.

"No, she's had lots of practice over the years. There's not much that spooks her, including dead animals or gunshots. She may look silly with those big ears, but she's really smart."

Will rode Sky behind Don. "Hey, Dad, I thought you had to go back to Schafer and contact Fish and Game."

Don turned in his saddle and leaned one hand on Tigger's back so he could face Will. He rocked gently in the saddle. "I do, but we're just about to Scott Lake and it's lunchtime. Think I'll have a bite with you before I head back."

At Scott Lake we tied up our horses and Babe, with her load of evidence. We grabbed our lunches from our saddlebags. I started to say something about how Scott Lake was such a great name because it was the same as my last name when a tall guy stumbled out of the woods about 50 feet from us. His clothes were torn and he carried a huge, heavy-looking backpack.

Dad spoke in a low voice. "What do you make of him?"

Don peered in the guy's direction. "Don't know, Tom. Let's see what he's got to say."

The man looked about 20. He had scratches on his face and hands. His brown hair stood up in every direction, as if it hadn't been combed in ages. He walked slowly toward us with his head down.

Dad called to him. "Hey, there! Are you all right?"

The man jumped. "Oh! Sorry. Didn't know anyone was here."

I couldn't tell if he looked confused or wary, but he didn't look happy to see us.

"Where ya headed?" Dad asked.

"Schafer Meadows."

"Were you camped at Flotilla Lake?"

Looking away, the man said, "No. I'm on my way to Schafer Meadows, like I said."

Don said, "How'd you get here if you didn't come from Flotilla Lake? You're nowhere near Schafer Meadows."

The man looked at his feet. "I came from the Morrison Creek Trail and camped somewhere along there last night near a stream. I thought I was on the trail to Schafer today but I ended up at a long lake. The trail dead-ended there." He pointed in the direction farther up the trail. "Is that what you're calling Flotilla Lake?"

Will, Allie, and I looked at each other. Was this guy for real?

Don stared at the man. "How'd you get those scratches?"

"I tripped on a rock in the trail and fell headfirst into an alder bush. Lost one of my water bottles. I spent half an hour looking for it down the hill but never did find it. Can you show me the way to Schafer?"

Dad got out his map, walked up to the man, and stuck out his hand. "Glad to help. I'm Tom Scott, the wilderness ranger at Schafer Meadows. This is Don and Will Lightner, Allie Carter, and my daughter, Jessie. The dogs are Oriole and Casey."

The man's face brightened and he stuck out his hand in return. "You're the ranger at Schafer? Hey, talk about luck! I'm Lou Wells. You know Cody Gray on the Schafer trail crew? He's a good friend of mine. I'm on my way to visit him."

Don continued to look at Lou's scratches. "If you're going to Schafer, how did you get on the other side of the Middle Fork

River from the Morrison Creek Trail? You don't cross the river to get to the ranger station."

"I didn't know I crossed it. There were some large creeks along Morrison. Now that you mention it, there was one that seemed a lot wider and deeper than the others. Must have been the river."

"See anyone else since you left the Morrison trailhead yesterday?"

"Yeah. A man on a horse pulling a mule passed me this morning near here. He's the only one, though."

"Did you talk to him?"

"I tried but he didn't want to talk much. He did say that he'd spent the night at a lake—must have been Flotilla 'cause it's the only one past here."

"Did you get his name?" Don asked.

"No. Like I said, he didn't talk much. He seemed to want to get going. After a couple of minutes we went our separate ways."

Lou undid the wide belt on his huge backpack. He rolled the backpack off one shoulder and down to one knee, and let it slide to the ground. Oriole and Casey immediately sniffed it.

"You must have something in your pack that smells pretty strong," I said. "Those dogs sure are interested in something in there."

Lou fidgeted. He cleaned his fingernails with a knife blade as he watched the dogs going over his pack. Then he sighed. "Guess I'd better be straight with you. I didn't want to tell you this 'cause it's embarrassing. But I need to take a break, so might as well."

He folded his knife and sat on the ground next to his pack. "The truth is I got lost. I always get lost. I've been to see Cody at Schafer a couple of times and each time I got lost. He and the others on the trail crew just laugh at me. They call me 'Lost Lou' or just 'Lost.' The name has stuck. Now you see why

I'm here and why it's so embarrassing. I haven't a clue how to get to Schafer. You have no idea how glad I am that you came along."

"Don't you carry a map?" Allie asked. She seemed to feel sorry for him.

"Sure, but reading a map to me is like trying to understand a foreign language I've never heard. It's gibberish."

"Why don't you travel with someone else?" I asked.

"Believe it or not, even though I get lost, I love being alone. There are lots of sounds—birds, water, animals, that sort of thing—that I might not hear hiking with someone else. I can go at my own pace and don't have to stick to anyone else's timetable. I can stay as long as I want and go wherever I want." He laughed. "If I can get there, that is."

"Is that why your pack's so heavy?" Don asked.

"That's it. There's enough food in my pack to feed an army. If I'm gonna get lost, at least I won't starve."

"What's in there that the dogs like so much?"

"Probably beef jerky from my lunch. Cody likes my homemade jerky, so I brought enough for us to have when we go backpacking. Want to try some? It's pretty good, if I do say so myself."

Dad shook his head. "You'd better make sure those bags are sealed tightly. Don't want to attract any other sniffing critters on your way to Schafer. Do you have a way to secure your food better?"

"Yeah," Lost Lou said. "My backpack's got a container inside for all my food. It's just that I took out the jerky to eat and left the bag out in case I wanted more. Guess I should take better care."

"Well, if you need more help on how to protect your food, stop to see us at Schafer Meadows or talk more to Cody. Here, let me show you how to get to Schafer. You'd probably like to get there before supper."

Dad gave instructions to Lou, using Lou's own map. He told him that on official maps, like those made by the U.S. government, the top is always north and the left side is always west. He showed him where we were and how to reach Schafer before sending him on his way.

Don took off his white straw cowboy hat, revealing sandy hair that matched Will's. He wiped sweat off his forehead with one sleeve of his sage green Forest Service shirt, and put his hat back on. Watching Lou walk away, he said, "That's one strange guy."

THREE

A Poaching Lesson

Dad watched Lou, too. "Do you think he's on the level?"

Don shrugged. "Don't know. That's a pretty weird tale to tell a bunch of strangers, but it'd be hard to make up something like that."

"Cody's a pretty good guy. I'd think he'd choose his friends well."

"Hey," I said. "You don't think he's the poacher, do you?"

Don shook his head. "I doubt it, but he's in the area at the right time. And he's got a heavy pack full of what he said is beef jerky that drove Oriole and Casey nuts."

"Shouldn't you have searched him, Dad?" Will asked.

"There's no reason to search him at this point. It's best for us to just stay aware of who's around and what they're doing. I'll try to learn more about him when I get back to Schafer and can talk to his friend Cody."

Allie cleaned her glasses on her T-shirt. "I hope he's okay. He seemed nice."

Dad reached into his saddlebag. "How 'bout we eat," he said. "I'm starved."

I opened my foil package that held cold grilled chicken and ate hungrily.

When we finished lunch, Dad folded his paper lunch sack and leaned back on his hands. "Don and I have an idea. How'd you like to go to Flotilla Lake for the night instead of staying here? It's only a little farther."

Will jumped up. "It's a great lake, Jessie and Allie. You'll love it. The views from there are awesome."

I'd only lived at Schafer Meadows a few weeks, so this was a new place for me to visit. "What's holding us up?" I asked. "Let's go."

Dad waved his hands in front of him. "Whoa. Hang on a minute. Don's got to get back to Schafer, and how 'bout we let Allie catch some fish for supper before we go? That's why you wanted to come here in the first place."

"First one to catch a fish doesn't have to cook dinner tonight," Allie said. She grabbed her fly rod and was off.

Don left for Schafer with the poached deer. The rest of us spent a couple of hours fishing marshy Scott Lake. Oriole and Casey swam and dozed in the sun while we walked along the shoreline. Allie caught the first fish, but Dad caught more fish than anyone else. We should have made him the winner. It would have been easier than watching Allie act like royalty. But it was all in fun.

"How'd you learn to fly fish, Allie?" Dad asked as we got ready to leave for Flotilla Lake. "That's a skill that takes a long time to learn, and I think it's really hard to fish Scott Lake because of all the marshy grasses."

Allie put her fly rod back in its case and loaded it onto her white horse, Lily. "My dad's loved fly fishing all his life. He taught my mom to fish. They used to go on fishing trips all over the country before we kids came along. It was just natural for them to teach us. My sister, brother, and I have all fished since we could hold a rod. Dad was into it so much that he now owns his own fly shop. Guess you could say it's in my blood."

"So what were you using as flies?"

"Dry flies—royal coachmen, mosquitoes, and grasshoppers. Today, that is. It all varies with the day and the water."

"You seem to know your stuff pretty well," Dad said. "Maybe someday you can give me lessons."

"I'd love to. Next to fishing, I like talking about fishing. I've never taught anyone, but I could try."

Cool, I thought. *Getting Dad to like Allie may mean I'll see more of her.*

I liked that a lot.

Finally Dad said we should ride to Flotilla Lake so there'd be time to enjoy the rest of the afternoon. We saddled up and turned up the trail.

We rode higher and higher to Flotilla Lake. The trail went through a swath of medium-sized lodgepole pine, Douglas-fir, and spruce trees before dropping down a long hill to the lake. Flotilla Lake looked like a spearhead, with a long flat end at the outlet and a pointed tip at the head. It sat in what Dad called a "cirque" basin, like "circle," a big rounded area at the base of a huge rocky ridge formed by ancient glaciers. One side along the lake was steep and heavily forested. The other was less steep but still had lots of trees. Clear blue-green water lapped at the edge of the lake where we made camp.

Allie and Dad tied a rope high between two trees to make a "highline," where they attached the lead ropes of the horses. They fished and watched the horses while Will and I hiked up the treeless ridge at the end of the lake to a small pond. Oriole and Casey cooled off in the water before we went back down to our camp. We got Red and Sky and rode up another slope to look down on Bradley Lake and the Middle Fork River a couple miles beyond. By the time we left there, our stomachs were growling.

Dad stir-fried veggies in a heavy skillet on the portable gas stove. He added pasta and pesto sauce made with basil, garlic, olive oil, and parmesan cheese. With the fish Allie and Dad caught, we had a huge feast.

After washing dishes in two plastic dishpans, I went to my tent and brought out my sleeping pad. It has side straps that snap together to turn the pad into a ground chair. It was way more comfortable than sitting on the cold gravelly ground. Oriole lay next to me, and I stroked her head and back as we watched Dad haul a bucket of sand from the beach and set it on the ground.

"Whatcha doin', Dad?" I asked.

"I'm making a fire blanket."

"A what?" Allie asked.

Dad showed us what looked like a piece of foil about two feet square. He spread it open on the ground and poured the beach sand on top.

"A fire blanket is made of any material that won't burn when a fire is built on top of it," he said. "When the fire goes out, we can take the cold ashes and bits of charcoal left on the blanket into the woods and scatter them so they don't leave a black scar on the ground. Then we can get clean sand from the lakeshore and spread it around where we built our campfire. No one will ever know it was here."

"Hey, that's pretty cool," Will said. "It makes me feel like no one's been here before me."

"Me, too," I said. "I bet others do, too."

"Plus, it's pretty easy," Allie said.

Earlier Dad had asked us kids to gather small twigs and sticks no larger around than our arms. He opened a small metal tube, took out a waterproof match, and struck it to a pile of twigs on the fire blanket. We smelled sulfur from the match until the crackling flames caught hold, first on small twigs and then on larger sticks. The little fire came to life. The comforting smell of a campfire filled the air. Soon we could feel its warmth. Dusk turned to night and the stars appeared one by one.

Dad said we didn't need to have a large fire, because a small one would keep us warm. Watching the flames flicker a golden color against the faces of my dad, the dogs, and my friends, I realized he was right. We were plenty warm and content by our little fire.

Casey, who had been sniffing around the campsite, yawned, stretched, and lay down next to Will. Dad must have caught Casey's bug, because he yawned, stretched, and eased deeper into his sleeping pad chair. He said, "I'm sorry you kids had to see the poached deer. I hope there won't be more."

Allie placed a small stick on the fire. "Does it happen often—poaching, I mean?"

"More often than you might think. What do you kids know about poaching?"

Allie shook her head. "I know people sometimes kill animals illegally but that's all."

"We talked about it some in school," Will said, "and I've heard some stories from my dad."

I thought about the deer. "Dad, you taught me about poaching when you worked for the Forest Service in New Mexico. It's a pretty ugly business. You said it happens all over. Like people even kill elephants in Africa just for their ivory tusks."

"Right. And it doesn't only happen in the forest or jungle. Poachers kill animals right in the middle of small towns and big cities."

"How can that be?" Allie asked. "Do big cities have wild animals?"

Dad poked the fire. "Unfortunately, yes. As cities spread out, many animals get pushed out of their habitat—their homes. Sometimes an animal looking for a new place to live wanders into a residential area and gets into trouble. They've even seen deer, bobcats, and coyotes in large cities like Los Angeles."

"We've had problems where I live in the Flathead Valley with deer, elk, moose, and even bears getting into birdseed, garbage, apples from orchards, and gardens," Will said. "And they're sometimes killed because they do."

"But why should they be killed?" Allie asked. "It's not their fault. They're only trying to find something to eat and a place to live like everybody else."

"You're right," Dad said. "But animals are usually the ones who lose. They're considered a nuisance. Some animals, like bears, pose a threat to people or their pets."

"That's pretty unfair," Allie said. "The animals were there first."

"It may be unfair, but that's what happens. And poachers take advantage of these situations any way they can."

I thought again about the dead deer. "But why do they poach in the first place?"

"For lots of reasons. Sometimes people need food, sometimes they want money and get paid well for hides or animal parts, and sometimes they just like to kill. But for whatever reason, they'll break any rule. And they can be extremely dangerous if you get in their way."

Dad chunked a piece of wood on the fire. "And don't think poachers all look like outlaws or weirdos. Your neighbor may be a poacher, or your minister, or the sheriff of your town. Poachers come from all over. They think they're above the law. Don't ever mess with a poacher. If you even think you see one, get out of there fast and get help."

"What's going to happen to the deer Don took as evidence?" I asked.

"He'll call Fish and Game. They're responsible for all poaching incidents. They'll send a game warden to investigate."

I felt better knowing someone wouldn't get away with killing the deer. What a lousy thing to do to an innocent animal. I also remembered what Dad said about poachers being dangerous. Oriole lay curled up by my side. Would a poacher harm her? Probably, if she got in his way. If poachers don't respect wildlife, why would they treat a pet any differently?

Suddenly I got scared. Oriole had saved me from more than one bad situation. I knew she wouldn't hesitate to get between me and a poacher if she thought I was in danger. I vowed to keep Oriole close to me so she'd be safe. That was my job.

The Backpackers

Normally Schafer Meadows is a flurry of activity. Workers give information and help to campers, river floaters, and outfitters who bring "dudes" or clients on wilderness trips, and provide emergency assistance. The trail crew fills the bunkhouse when they are not elsewhere building and maintaining hiking and horse trails. When we arrived back from our trip early the next afternoon, Schafer Meadows looked deserted. The ranger's house, cookhouse, bunkhouse, and barn silently faced the grassy airstrip in a half circle. The Middle Fork of the Flathead River flowed behind quietly, and high mountains of fir and pine surrounded the dark brown log buildings as if hiding a secret.

No one came to greet us as we neared the ranger's house—my house—and no one came out of the towering two-story cookhouse. Dad took our horses to the barn so we kids could get lunch in the cookhouse.

Allie looked slyly at Will and me. "I hear there's ice cream in the freezer. First one to the cookhouse door gets waited on by the other two."

With that she took off running. Will and I raced to catch her, but her long legs got her there first.

Oriole and Casey lay curled up outside the door with their eyes closed, but they weren't asleep. They raised their heads and looked expectantly at us, probably hoping someone would greet them with a treat. Allie patted them on the head.

"And you can find something for my furry friends while you're at it, now that I'm the queen." Allie went into the cookhouse kitchen and plunked down on a chair. "I'm sure they'd love some ice cream, too."

Will laughed. "They'd love anything put in front of them if it has to do with food. But no ice cream. They can have something else."

Oriole and Casey contented themselves with dog biscuits from Oriole's treat jar. It looks like a little white dog with a large black spot on its back. When you lift its head to get a treat it barks. Allie and Will laughed like crazy at that. The dogs stared at the jar until we gave them another biscuit.

We ate our sandwiches before I ran downstairs to the basement freezer and returned with a gallon of vanilla ice cream.

"I'll have lots of chocolate bits and peanuts in mine," Allie said, waving her hand like royalty.

Will picked up a bowl full of ice cream and held it menacingly over Allie's head. "I'll give you chocolate bits and peanuts."

The door opened. Charlie the station guard, a tall thin white-haired man with a white mustache and a red bandana around his neck, stopped abruptly. "Hey, what's going on? That doesn't look too friendly."

I grinned. "Don't worry, Charlie. Will was just about to crown Allie as queen."

"Not with that ice cream, you're not," Charlie said, grabbing the bowl from Will. He got a spoon, sat down next to Allie, and started eating. "Mmmm. Thanks for dessert. I was just coming in for some."

As the Schafer Meadows station guard, Charlie maintains the ranger station, keeps track of plane traffic at Schafer's small airstrip, monitors the Forest Service radio for messages, and usually knows where most people are during the day. He pays close attention to everything that happens. "Don says you found a poached deer. Tell me about it."

Will sat down next to Charlie. He dished out more ice cream, slid bowls to Allie and me, and frowned. He told Charlie about the deer.

I licked my spoon. "Hey, Charlie, do you know where Mom and my weird brother Jed are? We wanted to tell them about the deer."

"Jed and Pete are on their way back from packing out the trail crew's gear. Your mother's at the house, Jessie."

Will, Allie, and I washed our dishes, put them in the dish drainer, and went to the log cabin near the cookhouse. The squeaky screen door announced our arrival. Oriole and Casey squeezed past us into the living room.

Mom sat at her computer by the window, working on her latest historical romance novel, changing yet another battery because Schafer has no electricity. She could use a typewriter but says it takes way too long to write and edit her manuscripts.

Mom straightened her blonde ponytail under her baseball cap, sat back from her computer, and smiled. "I didn't expect you for a few hours. How was your trip?"

We told her about the deer, meeting Lost Lou Wells, fishing, and camping.

"Well, I'm glad you three are having fun. What's up now? Why don't you go fishing along the river or something?"

I grabbed my baseball cap, tucking my blonde hair out the back in a ponytail like Mom's. "Yeah, that's not a bad idea. Hey, Mom, do you think Will and Allie will have to leave? Because of the deer, I mean?"

"I don't know, Jessie. Don and Allie's parents have to make that decision."

We decided to take Mom's advice and fish along the river. We hiked the Big River Trail past the campground about

¼-mile to a junction with the Schafer Creek Trail where it drops down to the Middle Fork River.

Will had brought a small daypack rather than a fishing rod. He sat cross-legged next to the river and took out a sketch pad and pencils from his pack.

I looked over his shoulder. "Wow, Will. Did you do that?"

A mountain scene in colored pencils filled a page in his sketchbook. A river snaked through the middle of it. A person on horseback pulled a pack string of nine mules that splashed through the water. The scene looked real.

Will grabbed a brown pencil and a fresh sheet of paper. "I did that when Dad took me on a trip last summer. We watched a packer take his string across the river. It was so cool. I had to draw it."

I baited my line and glanced once more at the drawing. "You're really good, Will. I can't wait to see this new one when it's done."

"I'm making a map of all the places we visit on this trip," he said. "So far I've got Schafer Meadows, Scott and Flotilla lakes, the Middle Fork River, and the Morrison Creek Trail to put on. I don't think I can face the map to the north, though. It would look too crowded."

Oriole and Casey swam as Allie and I fished along the gravelly bank. Allie caught two big trout with her new fly rod, which made her happy, but I got skunked with my casting rod and worm bait. It felt good just enjoying the warm sun and listening to the river roll over rocks as it moved past us. By mid-afternoon we'd had enough. We took Allie's fish, went back for Will, and walked slowly back up the trail from the river. Oriole and Casey, soaked and smelling like wet dogs, trotted ahead, bumping each other like friends.

When we reached the trail junction, we saw a lone rider on the Big River Trail, going toward the horse camp, about a mile upriver from Schafer. His back was to us. He rode a tall chestnut horse and led a big black mule carrying fat canvas manty packs.

"He's the first stranger I've seen in a couple of days," I said, as we turned back toward the ranger station. "Wonder where he came from?"

We found Dad with Jed and Pete, Dad's assistant, in the cookhouse basement. They had returned from packing out the trail crew from their camp. Unopened bundles of white canvas manty tarps still tied with the thick ropes that secure them to pack mules leaned like dominoes against the basement door to the cookhouse. Other manties lay spread open on the floor with wooden boxes on them. They held tents, work boots, hard hats, gloves, and clothes waiting for crew members to retrieve.

Jed looked up as he hunkered over an unwrapped manty, fiddling with the rope to untie it. The sun caught his blue eyes, which were puffy. Jed looked tired and ornery. "Hey, twerps, how was your campout?"

"Great, dork. How was your trip packing out the crew?" I said, looking at all the gear. "Looks like you had a busy time."

Sweat dripped off Jed's nose as he smiled and nodded. He took off his black cowboy hat. His black hair was soaked. He wiped the sweat with the tail of his tan cowboy shirt, which hung out from his jeans. Jed coiled a rope from one of the manties and wrapped the outside end of the rope around and around. He put the end through the strands of rope at the top to secure it and hung it next to others on a post nail awaiting use on the next pack trip.

"Heard you found a poached deer up toward Scott Lake," Jed said.

"Yeah," I said. "Unlike you, we keep our eyes open on the trail. It's amazing what you can see. Hey, Dad. Any word from Don?"

Dad folded the last of the manties and put them in a corner of the basement. "Yep. Don said the game warden is on his way. Should be here anytime now."

"How's he getting here so fast?"

"He's flying in. This is a pretty serious offense, so the warden wants to get right on it."

Thinking of planes made me long for my tall silver-haired pilot friend, Jim, one of my favorite people at Schafer Meadows. He actually lives in Kalispell but flies into Schafer to see Charlie from time to time. They're old friends. Jim loves Oriole, so that makes him my friend, too. He often brings Oriole gifts. Recently he gave her a red collapsible dog bowl. She ate and drank out of it on our overnight trip to Flotilla Lake.

"Dad, do you think Jim will visit us soon?" I asked.

"I don't know, Jessie. We'll see."

"Oh, I hope he does. I miss him."

Will looked out the basement door. "Hey, does anyone know where my dad is?"

Jed coiled another manty rope and tossed it to Pete. "Check out our house. He was headed that way."

Oriole and Casey ran to the back of the house while we went inside. Mom was still pounding computer keys. Will asked about his dad.

"He's putting up a wall tent behind our house," Mom said. "I think he plans to stay a while. You're still welcome to sleep in Jed's bedroom if you want, Will, or you can camp out with your dad and the game warden."

Will wrinkled his nose. "Do we have to sleep on the ground in the tent?"

Mom laughed. "No, not at all. Don—uh, your dad—put up cots for the three of you."

"Good. I don't mind sleeping on the ground—I do it all the time when camping—but having a cot is kind of a treat in the backcountry. I'll probably stay with my dad and the game warden if that's okay."

"What about me, Kate?" Allie asked. "Can I still sleep on the sofa in your living room?"

Hearing Allie call my mom by name still sounded strange, even though I call adults by their first name all the time around Schafer Meadows. Even Don, Will's dad. It's just the way things are done in the backcountry. We live so close together that everyone's like family, so it's natural.

Mom nodded. "I'm sorry you can't stay in Jessie's room with her, but as you saw, it's too small for more than one person. You're welcome to stay with us on the fold-out couch as long as you're here. I know Jessie would like it."

Allie made a small hop. "Thanks. I don't mind sleeping on a cot or the ground, but a sofa bed in a warm wilderness cabin is a luxury to me. You can have your old cot, Will."

From a distance came the drone of a small plane. I went outside to watch it. It circled the grassy airstrip once and then came back to land. The plane, blue on top and white below, taxied to the pole fence. My eyes got big and I and ran toward the airstrip. "Hey, you guys!" I shouted over my shoulder. "It's Jim!"

The small plane's propeller stopped and two men stepped out from the plane. A tall well-built pilot with silver hair and a blue baseball cap opened the back seat. He took out a duffel bag and other gear and dropped it on the ground. Oriole raced ahead of me and ran to the pilot. The man knelt down and grabbed Oriole's head in his hands affectionately as she tried to lick his face. When I reached him he stood up, spread his arms wide, and gave me a huge hug.

"Oh, Jim! It's great to see you," I said. Oriole circled him, beating herself with her tail as it wagged back and forth.

"Looks like Oriole missed you, too."

Jim looked around with a big smile. "Well, it's great to be back."

About that time everybody else got there, including Charlie, who had been inside the cookhouse. Jim shook hands all around, scratched Casey on the head, and slapped his friend Charlie on the back a couple of times. "I'd like all of you to meet someone," he said.

A man of medium height with a stocky build smiled at us.

"This is Carlos Sanchez, the game warden," Jim said. "He's here to investigate the poached deer."

The man had a dark complexion and black eyes, hair, and mustache. "Pleased to meet you," he said. He shook all of our hands except Mom's. He tipped his black cowboy hat to her and called her "ma'am."

Mom looked surprised but said, "Please. Call me Kate."

The man smiled and nodded. "And please, all of you call me Carlos." He spoke with a slight Hispanic accent, like some of my friends in Silver City, New Mexico, where I used to live. I wondered if Carlos came from anywhere near there.

"We can take your things to the upstairs room at the back of the cookhouse, Carlos," Dad said. "You can bunk there if you'd like."

"Thanks," Carlos said. "But when Don called, he said there'd be a spot for me in a wall tent with him and Will. That'll work just fine."

"Well, okay then. After you get settled we'll tell you what little we know of the poaching incident. Jed, why don't you help Carlos with his gear?"

"Sure thing, Dad." Jed grabbed the duffel bag and gear from the ground, hoisted the duffel on his shoulder, and headed off to the wall tent next to our house.

The others left for the cookhouse.

I stayed with Jim. "Where are you staying, Jim?"

"In the campground, my home away from home."

"I'll help you take your stuff there," I said.

Jim opened the passenger door on the plane. "Hop in, Jessie. We'll taxi to the end of the runway so I can tie this baby down near the campground."

When the plane was shut off and Jim unloaded his tent and gear, I tried to carry Jim's duffel. It took both hands, and even then the bag almost dragged on the ground. Jim put his hand on my arm to stop me.

"Here, let me take that. I've got something else for you to carry." He handed me a paper bag containing a small square box. "Open it," he said with a sly grin.

I opened the box and pulled out a small black headset like some pilots wear, except it didn't have a microphone attached. I turned it around in my hands and gave Jim a shrug. It was definitely too small for me.

Jim scratched Oriole on the head. "Remember when we flew the first time and talked about Oriole and how much stronger her sense of hearing is than ours? You were afraid the loud noise of the plane's engine might hurt her ears. This is for her. I found it on the Internet. If she'll wear it, it should give her good hearing protection when she flies."

"Oh, Jim, that's incredible!" I said. I knelt down and put the headset on Oriole. She lowered her head and pulled it off with her paw. She looked ashamed when we laughed.

"Looks like I've got to work on getting her to wear it," I said. "But if I know her she'll keep it on after a while, especially when she realizes how much it cuts the noise."

I slung Jim's tent roll under my arm, carried the box and headset, and walked with a light step to the campground.

While Jim set up camp, Oriole and I left for the cookhouse. Loud talk escaped from inside. I could barely squeeze in through the screen door. The large kitchen was jammed with people fixing a snack at the counter next to the huge silver gas cook stove and oven. At Schafer Meadows, we eat family-style in the big cookhouse kitchen. Sometimes it gets pretty noisy and crowded, but I have some of the best times at meals because of all the people.

Will and Allie laughed at some joke that Pete told, probably something to do with the last project Dad gave him. Pete's over six feet tall. His huge hands were wrapped around a double-decker roast beef and cheese sandwich. Some snack. His brown eyes caught mine, and he smiled.

"Hey, Jessie, your friends here say you're lousy at catching fish."

Pete practically had to shout for me to hear him over the other voices in the room.

"Yeah, well, I'm still better than you."

"Oh, yeah? Some day your friends and I will have to see if that's true."

I was about to reply when another voice caught my attention.

"Hey, Jessie—how ya doin'?"

I turned around. "Celie, how are you? Dad said you guys just got back from your trail project. It's great to see you."

A tall thin young woman with dark skin and black hair worn in a single braid down her back gave me a big hug. She wore a beaded bracelet with a brightly-colored zigzag pattern and small black-and-white beaded feathers.

I put down my granola bar and reached for her wrist to look closer at the bracelet. "Wow! Is this a Blackfeet design? It's beautiful."

"It is. My mother does some of the Blackfeet Nation's finest beadwork."

Celie Long Runner, the trail crew leader for Schafer Meadows, put her hands on the back of Will and Allie's chairs.

"I remember you two. You're Jessie's friends. I know she's glad you're here. We 'old' people just don't have the same appeal to her."

"That's right," said another young woman who moved next to Celie. She had bushy brown hair loosely tied with an orange cloth-covered rubber band. "We try, though."

Mandy Lake was easy to talk to and had this great smile that I'd love to have. "Hey, you'd like the trail we're working on," Mandy said. "Maybe you and your friends can come visit us when we go back to work."

"Really? We could visit? I'll ask Dad. Maybe we could help on your project," I said. "By the way, where's Cody?"

Celie and Mandy looked at each other and laughed. "He's with his friend, Lou Wells. Remember him? The guy everyone calls 'Lost?' He said he ran into you at Scott Lake when he was trying to get to Schafer."

Dad, who sat at the far end of the table with Don and Warden Carlos, said, "Did he finally make it here?"

"Yeah," Celie said. "He got here when you were at Flotilla Lake. He looked pretty relieved to be here. I can't believe the way he gets lost all the time."

Don grabbed the lemonade pitcher as it went around the table. "Have you known him long?"

"He's been here a couple of times to see Cody. They always go off backpacking somewhere. I think Lost likes those trips because he can count on Cody to get him wherever they're going and back again. They went off for a walk a little while ago to talk and plan their next trip."

Celie and Mandy laughed again.

"So Lost is a pretty good guy?" Dad asked.

"Yeah, he's pretty harmless as far as we can tell," Mandy said as she sat at the long table.

Pete picked up what was left of his giant sandwich with his huge hands and took a bite. "Lost and Cody have known each other since high school," Pete said through a mouthful of sandwich. "I think Cody said they're best friends."

"Well, I hope they get back soon," Don said. "I'd like Lou—uh, Lost—to talk to Warden Carlos about whether he saw the deer carcass near Scott Lake."

Oriole barked. Her tail wagged as she looked outside the door. Casey barked with her. We heard voices and then someone yoo-hooed. Two men and two women who looked like college students stood outside away from the door and the dogs.

Mom was closest to the door. She opened it. "Oriole! Casey! It's okay. Let them by."

To the four visitors, she said, "Come on in. If you can, that is. We're pretty crowded at the moment."

Everyone standing moved to the table so the others could come inside.

"We didn't mean to interrupt," said a man of medium height. He wore a faded red bandana over short, curly, light brown hair that looked like he hadn't washed it in days. His jeans were torn at the knees, and he had on an old green T-shirt with grease and brown stains all over it. "We're backpacking and wanted to ask you about some of the trails in the area."

"No problem," Dad said. "That's what we're here for. Grab a seat."

The man sat across from Dad on the long bench against the wall. "I'm Wiley, but my friends call me Coyote."

"How 'bout some lemonade?" Mom said. "It's not fresh-squeezed, but it'll do on a hot day."

A woman with red hair and freckles sat down next to Coyote. He put his arm around her waist. She reached for Mom's offered glass with a dirty hand. "That sounds wonderful. We've been drinking water for so long that anything flavored would taste good. By the way, I'm Emma."

"And I'm Tracy," said an athletic-looking woman wearing an ankle-length skirt, a peasant blouse, and hiking boots and socks. She patted the seat next to her. The last man sat down.

"My name's Steve. Great place you've got here," he said with a New York accent. "This is my first time in the woods, let alone a wilderness."

It looked that way. Steve wore jeans and a T-shirt—good enough for Schafer—but instead of high-quality hiking boots he had on a cheap pair of hiking shoes that I'd seen in discount stores. He looked like he was nursing a blister on one foot.

"Are you planning to be out long?" Dad asked.

"We've got the rest of the summer to explore the wilderness," Coyote said. "We'll have to go out on occasion to get more supplies, but we don't have to be back to college until fall."

"How long have you been in the Great Bear Wilderness?" Don asked.

Coyote's eyes fell to Don's Forest Service badge and nametag. "About two weeks now."

"Have you run into many other people?"

"Not many. We've seen an outfitter group, a guy traveling alone with a horse and mule, and a couple of people fishing the river. That's about it."

I thought of the guy we'd seen riding toward the horse camp. I got pretty excited. "Hey, was the lone guy on horseback tall, and did he have big animals?"

"Yeah, that's right," Tracy said, refilling her glass with lemonade.

"When did you see him?"

Tracy looked at Steve. "What do you think, a week or more?"

Steve took a big swallow and set his empty glass back on the table. "Yeah, I guess so. The days start to blend together after a while."

"We saw him along the Middle Fork River, so that must have been about a week and a half ago," Emma said.

"Which way was he headed?" Don asked.

"Upriver, I think. Why, you looking for him?" Coyote asked.

"Nope. Just curious. He seems to be around a lot but no one's met him yet."

Everyone finished their snack. Dad went into the little office in the back of the kitchen and brought out a map. He spent the next ten minutes showing the four backpackers different trails out of Schafer. Then they got up to leave.

"Thanks for the information," Emma said as they walked to the door. "And for the lemonade. We're setting up in the campground tonight. Come visit if you have time."

I thought I saw Coyote give Emma a dirty look. Maybe he didn't want us kids hanging around with them. Jed sometimes gets like that when I'm with him and his friends.

After they left, Warden Carlos asked to speak to Dad, Don, and Pete about the poached deer. We kids wandered outside. Casey and Oriole jumped up and came with us, looking hopeful that they might get to do something fun. I watched the four grungy people we'd just met walk with heavy backpacks toward the campground. The one guy Steve limped along way behind the other three. His blister must have really hurt.

We kids ran to the airstrip to throw balls for the dogs. At the far end, just going out of sight to the west, I thought I saw a tall man on horseback with a tall mule carrying a very heavy load. If that was the same guy we saw while fishing earlier today, that was sure a quick trip! I blinked and he was gone.

Was I dreaming?

FIVE

The Cub

After lunch the next day I whistled for Oriole and we kids
hiked to the horse camp, a mile up the Big River Trail from
the campground. Will and I had been there before, but it was
new to Allie. I had seen an osprey there one day and hoped to
get another glimpse of it through my binoculars. I also knew
Oriole would have fun swimming in the Middle Fork River that
runs along the south edge of the camp.

The trail goes past the campground, past the junction to
the Schafer Creek Trail, and into a tunnel of lodgepole pine that
forms a dark canopy. It's wide and flat and mostly dirt, unlike
the trails I hiked in New Mexico, where cobbles the size of
grapefruits made walking slow and difficult. Here, tall grasses
on either side of the trail hid Oriole from time to time as she
wandered back and forth, back and forth. With no good view of
the mountains to catch our attention, we just talked and walked
along.

"Hey Will, do you miss Casey?" I asked.

"Yeah," he said, adjusting the small green day pack he
wore on his back. "A lot. Sometimes I forget he's Dad's law
dog. When Dad needs him to help on a case, like today, I feel
like I'm missing something or forgot something."

"I know what you mean. I feel the same about Oriole. And
without her best friend, Oriole looks kinda lonesome, too."

Casey's job comes first, which Oriole didn't seem to
know. When Casey left with Don earlier, I had to call Oriole
back. Her ears and tail drooped as her friend got farther from
sight.

At the junction with the trail to the horse camp, we heard
bawling. We stopped so we could hear better. It didn't sound
human—more a nasal WAAAHHH—but it was hard to tell
what it was. To be safe, I kept Oriole by my side.

The mournful wails continued until we saw a tiny black
bear waddle out of the forest onto the Big River Trail about a
hundred feet ahead, moving away from us. It kept walking and
bawling, looking from side to side.

"Look at that little cub," Allie whispered. "It can't be very
old. Why's it crying?"

"It must be calling its mother," Will said quietly. "Wonder
where she is?"

Oriole had her ears forward and her eyes focused on the
little bear. Her leg muscles trembled as she watched the cub
wander farther up the trail and amble back into the forest above
the horse camp. She whined softly.

I knelt down and put my arm around her. "Shhhhh," I said.
"We don't want to scare the poor thing. I don't think it knows
we're here."

Will went off the trail a few feet and sat behind the biggest pine around, which wasn't very big. He glanced up the
trail toward the cub. "We'd better wait here awhile. No telling
where the mother is, and we don't want to mess with her,
especially since she's got a cub. Mother bears with cubs can be
really dangerous."

I looked around, hoping to spot the mother. "We learned
in New Mexico that you can get into a lot of trouble if you
get between a bear and her cub. If the mother thinks you're a
threat, she might attack."

We folded our legs and sat behind Will's tree for about
five minutes, but after no sign of either the cub or its mother,
we went on.

At the big meadow in the horse camp, we heard voices.
Two men sat next to the river, leaning back with their hands

behind them on the ground. They dangled their feet in the
water. Oriole stood still for a minute with her head cocked and
then bolted toward them.

One of the men stood up. "Oriole! What are you doing
here?" He started wrestling with her. I almost didn't recognize
him without his black cowboy hat, but then I saw that he
looked a lot like my brother Jed.

"Cody!" I said. "What're you doing here? How come
you're not at Schafer with the rest of the trail crew?"

Cody kept playing with Oriole. "Hi, Jessie! My friend Lost
and I came here to catch up on things. Lost said he met you at
Scott Lake when he was trying to find his way to Schafer."

Cody stuck out his hand to Will and Allie. "I remember
you two. We met briefly at Schafer a couple weeks ago. I'm
Cody Gray, in case you forgot. I work on the trail crew. Guess I
don't have to introduce you to Lost."

Lost stood up and gave a shy smile. "Yeah, hi again. How
was your overnight trip?"

"Really great," Allie said, cleaning her round glasses on
her T-shirt. "We decided to camp at Flotilla Lake rather than at
Scott Lake. You should have come with us instead of going to
Schafer."

"Maybe someday. I gotta take advantage of Cody's knowl-
edge of the area, though. As long as I'm with him, I get to see
some great country."

I tossed a stick into the river, and Oriole dove in after it.
The stick drifted downstream. She raced to reach it, grabbed
it in her teeth, and swam back hard against the current. On the
shore, Oriole dropped the stick at my feet and started a slow
side-to-side shake. We all jumped back before she could pick
up speed and spray us with water.

"Hey," I said, tossing another stick into the river and
watching Oriole do a belly flop after it. "You guys didn't happen to see a bear cub here, did you? A little while ago we saw

one come out of the horse camp and head up the Big River
Trail calling for its mother."

"We did," Cody said. "Not long ago. We didn't see the
mother bear so we stayed here to give her some room."

"Do you think the cub could be lost?"

"I doubt it. The mother was probably somewhere nearby
and they're long gone by now. So, what's been going on the
past couple of days, Jessie? Get into any trouble?"

We told him about the poached deer we found. Cody
looked troubled. "Lost, we'd better get back to Schafer,"
he said. "I think we need to have Jessie's dad call the game
warden."

"He's already at Schafer," I said. "Why? What happened?"

"Nothing—maybe. The fact that we all saw the bear cub
without the mother doesn't necessarily mean anything. But,
you guys having seen the poached deer makes it a little ques-
tionable. I'd like to get someone else's opinion. That's all."

He and Lost put on their socks and boots and got their
backpacks.

"Let's go," he said and we followed him at a fast clip.

Back at Schafer, we stopped at the bunkhouse long
enough for Cody and Lost to drop their backpacks before going
to the cookhouse.

"Tom, are you here?" Cody called as we entered the
kitchen.

"In the office," Dad said from the back room. "Be there
shortly."

Dad and Charlie came out carrying maps. "What's up?"
Dad asked.

Cody grabbed a glass from the cupboard and filled it with
water from the sink. "Jessie said that Carlos, the game warden,
is here. We need to talk to him."

"He already knows about the deer. He and Pete went with Will's dad, Don, and Casey to look at the site."

"This isn't about the deer," Cody said, and he told Dad about the bear cub that he and Lost had seen. He also said they didn't see the mother.

"And that was before Will and Allie and I saw the cub," I said. "We never saw the mother, either, but the cub was crying and walking up the trail like it was trying to find her."

Dad walked to the kitchen door and looked outside. He put his hands in his pockets and blew out a deep breath. "Huh. I don't want to jump to conclusions, but that's not good."

Dad turned around and faced us again. "I gave Don a radio in case he needed to call us. Guess I'd better call him instead. Cody, can you and Lost stay here until Don and Warden Carlos get back?"

"Sure thing. That's what we had planned to do anyway. C'mon, Lost. I'll show you where you can bunk."

After they left, Dad radioed Don. Charlie kept us kids occupied by showing us his latest carvings. One was a bird with a fish in its mouth and another was a mountain lion. He reached up on top of the refrigerator and brought down a small block of wood with a few smoothed edges.

He ran his thumb over one of the edges. "This is my next project. I hope you like it, Jessie. It's for you."

"Gee, nice," I said, reaching for Charlie's project. "I always wanted a block of wood."

Charlie pulled his hand back. "Keep that up and I won't give it to you when it's done."

"What's it gonna be?"

Charlie's wood carvings could be put in a museum if you asked me, so I knew this would be good.

"You'll just have to wait and see."

Oriole stuck her nose in the air as far as she could, sniffed at Charlie's block of wood, and wagged her tail.

"Looks like Oriole thinks it's okay," Charlie said. "At least she knows fine art when she sees it."

We joked with Charlie for a while. He and my pilot friend Jim are like uncles to me—easy to talk to about anything and fun to be around. Will went to look for Jed, who promised to show him some packing techniques he'd learned from Pete. Allie, Oriole, and I left for my house to spend the rest of the afternoon listening to music from a new rock group Allie liked.

After dinner, I worked with Oriole, trying to get her to keep the headset on that Jim had given her. Each time, she either pawed it off or shook her head so it fell off. Finally she gave in and left it on. She put her head on the ground and let out a big sigh. I praised her and took the headset off. We played tug-o'-war with a rope toy. When I put the headset on her again, she looked less leery of it. We played some more, and the next time I put the headset on her, she left it on and walked around slowly. When I felt she had accepted wearing it, I asked Will and Allie if they wanted to go visit Jim in the campground with Oriole and me.

Jim sat in his camp chair reading a book. His silver hair shone in the sun from under his pilot's baseball cap.

"I've got a surprise for you, Jim," I said. "Watch this."

I put the headset on Oriole and she walked up to Jim and laid her head in his lap. Jim put his book on the small table attached to his camp chair and ruffled the fur along Oriole's back.

"Good dog, Oriole," Jim said. "You're all set to fly now."

Oriole wagged her tail and ran off to find a stick. The headset fell off her head and landed in the dirt. Jim laughed as he got out of his chair, picked up the device, and brushed it off.

"Guess these things aren't made for running around," he said as he handed it to me. "She should be fine in a plane where she's confined to her seat. We'll have to take her up for a spin sometime soon. Maybe we can all go."

"Wow," Allie said. Her eyes looked big behind her round glasses. "That would be cool."

"Yeah," Will said, "I love flying over the wilderness. It's so beautiful—no roads, only big skies, lots and lots of mountains, and deep forests. My favorite!"

"Well, we'll see what we can do about getting you up in the air sometime soon," Jim said. "I try not to fly more than I have to in the wilderness to help keep the number of flights down. But I may need to someday."

We visited a while longer with Jim and then the entire trail crew—Celie, Cody, and Mandy—showed up with Jed and Lost.

Celie twisted her beautiful beaded bracelet around her wrist with her hand. She looked toward the tents set up on the other side of the campground. The four backpackers we had met yesterday sat at a picnic table beside the tents eating their dinner.

"Think we should go see if they decided on a trip from here?" Celie said. "They talked a long time with Tom about which trails to take."

Lost grinned. "Anytime someone gives me information to keep me on the right track helps. Course it still doesn't mean I'll get to where I want to go."

"You couldn't find your way if every tree in the forest had a sign pointing you in the right direction," Cody joked.

A breeze blew Mandy's bushy hair. She pushed it away from her eyes. "Maybe Lost is right," she said. "We can at least ask if they've figured out where they're going."

Everyone but Jim walked to the backpackers' campsite. Wiley, the one called 'Coyote,' stood as we approached and stepped away from the table.

"Hey, how's it going?" Coyote asked, chewing on a piece of meat.

"Not bad," Jed said. "Sorry to interrupt your dinner."

"No problem. Grab a seat and join us. We've got plenty to eat."

None of us sat down, but Oriole worked her way around the table, wagging her tail and looking for handouts.

"Oriole, cut that out!" I said. "No begging!"

Tracy, who wore the long skirt and peasant blouse said, "Oh, she's all right." She held a piece of meat in Oriole's direction. "Can she have a bite?"

Oriole made a beeline for Tracy. I grabbed her collar before she had a chance to open her mouth and take the meat.

"No, but thanks. I'm trying to keep her from becoming a beggar. With all the people who visit Schafer Meadows, it's hard."

"Sure. I understand. Sorry, Oriole." Tracy pulled her hand back and continued eating. Oriole's eyes followed as Tracy's hand went up to her mouth and down to her plate. Drool seeped out of both sides of Oriole's mouth. I made her stand behind me so she couldn't watch Tracy.

Steve, the guy from New York, sat next to Tracy with one leg stretched out on the table bench. A bunched wool sock hung loosely on his toes, and a large bandage covered his ankle.

"What'd you do to your foot?" Cody asked. "It looks pretty sore."

Steve bent down and touched his wrapped ankle. "I got a pretty good-sized blister from wearing these shoes. I'm hoping the air will help it heal. Every step I take in those shoes is pretty painful right now. I don't know how I'm going to keep going."

"We've got first aid equipment in the cookhouse if you need anything."

Coyote walked over and stood by Steve. He folded his arms over his chest. "Thanks, but we've got a good first aid kit with moleskin."

"We've got some bandages with gels that might work better. They stick to the wound and might heal faster."

Coyote shot Cody a nasty look. "That's okay. We can take care of it."

Steve stared at Coyote and then looked away. He said, "Yeah. It'll be okay."

Celie stooped over to look at Steve's foot. "I wouldn't try hiking on that foot for a few days. Give it time to rest."

Emma sat across the table from Steve and Tracy. She gave a big nod. "That's what I keep telling Coyote. We need to wait here until Steve's foot heals enough for him to travel. But Coyote wants to go out tomorrow."

Coyote sat down, stabbed a piece of meat, and threw his fork on his plate. "We can't just hang around waiting for Steve's foot to heal. We've got business to attend to. You all knew that when we came in here."

Emma's face got almost as red as her hair. "Right, but this is different. Steve's foot could get infected."

"Emma's right," Tracy said quietly. "Steve needs to stay here. Tell you what, Coyote. Why don't you and I go out first thing tomorrow morning and we'll leave Emma and Steve here? I can travel as fast as you and carry nearly as much. We can meet the person you need to see, go to Kalispell to buy Steve a decent pair of hiking boots, and be back here in a couple days. I know it'd be better to have Steve try on his own boots, but we'll do our best to get him a pair that fits. It might be the best option for now. Emma can help take care of Steve while we're gone."

Coyote frowned, but at last he agreed. Emma put her arm around his neck and hugged him. "That's the right thing to do. Just hurry back. We'll miss you two."

"Look," Celie said. "We'll leave you alone, but if you need anything let us know. We'll be at Schafer for a couple more days before our next hitch—uh, our next work schedule—starts."

We kids split off from the trail crew to say goodnight to Jim. On our way back to my house, Oriole trotted ahead. When we got to the cookhouse, she looked confused not to find Casey there. She walked slowly with us.

"Guess she misses Casey as much as I do," Will said as he lifted the flap on his wall tent. "See ya in the morning."

Ben Morris

Mom patted Smurf, her small gray horse, and swung into her saddle. She nudged him forward with her foot. Allie rode Lily in front of Red and me. Will followed on Sky and led our mule, Kitty. Kitty carried all of our things except our raingear, which was tied behind our saddles, and the snacks and water we kept in our saddlebags. Jed rode last on Rocky in case Will needed help. Charlie waved goodbye as we left Schafer Meadows.

Mom's blonde ponytail, hanging out from behind her baseball cap, swayed in time to Smurf's tail as we rode up the Big River Trail. She raised her arms high and wide and looked toward the sky.

"Wow, what a day!" she said. "Look at those big puffy clouds and bright blue sky. Looks like we'll have good weather tonight."

Mom said she'd felt tied to her computer since we'd arrived at Schafer Meadows earlier in the summer. She loves writing historical romance novels, but sometimes it consumes all of her time and she needs to take a break from her work. This was one of those times.

She wanted to go on an overnight trip somewhere, and Jed suggested a small campsite he knew of near Cox Creek, about seven miles up the Big River Trail. We could ride there in the morning, hang out the rest of the day near the river, and ride back the next morning.

We left after breakfast. Oriole scouted the trail in front of us, trotting along with her tail high. Occasionally she lagged behind when an interesting scent on a bush or log caught her attention. Once in a while she'd stop too close to the trail for us to pass her safely. Mom patiently pulled Smurf to a halt, but Will wasn't as tolerant.

"C'mon, Oriole, move it," he said. "Kitty's half asleep this morning and keeps running into Sky. I don't want him to kick her and cause a wreck."

"Sorry," I said. "Oriole's really giving those branches a long sniff. She must have good mail to read this morning."

Oriole raced ahead. We rode up the Big River Trail past the deep basin below Chair Mountain and Gable Peaks. The tall sheer cliffs of Gable Peaks looked nearly white against the deep blue sky.

"Those peaks give me an idea for a book," Mom said. She took her left foot out of the stirrup, hooked her leg over the saddle horn, and sat sideways. She faced the cliffs and then looked over her shoulder at us.

"Oh, no, I can see it now," I said.

With a slow deliberate motion, I brought my hand to my cheek and said in a deep voice to someone unseen, "Ginger! Don't do it, Ginger. Get away from that cliff!"

My hands flew to my chest and I threw my head back. With a high-pitched voice, I said, "I must. You don't love me anymore, Gerald. Life holds no meaning for me."

"Ginger, no! Ginger!"

"Too late, Gerald, goodbye. Aaaaaahhhhhhh! Splat."

Mom shook her head and laughed. "You're bad, Jessie. You know that, don't you?"

"It's only because I love you, Mom. Who else do you have to help you write your award winners?"

"Okay, so help me write this story: Loving mother has a good son and a rotten misbehaving daughter...Hmmmm. Sounds vaguely familiar."

It felt good watching Mom loosen up. She works long hours writing and rewriting. She has a pretty good following of readers who buy her books, but she hasn't yet hit the big one. Someday.

A trail sign told us we were leaving the Great Bear Wilderness and crossing into the Bob Marshall—no bump in the trail, no change from forest to open space—just a sign. Finally we reached a meadow full of tall grasses and tons of wildflowers.

"Wow," Allie said. "It looks like every color of the rainbow must be here. I wish we could stay a while."

"We can," Jed said. "See that small trail heading down toward the river? That's where the campsite is."

"Great," Mom said. "This is perfect."

She turned Smurf down the narrow side trail. We rode through part of the meadow before entering a small campsite surrounded by dark green subalpine fir and spruce trees. Shade from the trees kept the sun's rays from reaching the ground except for a few open places where the sunshine covered the forest floor like splattered pale yellow paint. A small breeze blew. I closed my eyes and inhaled deeply. It smelled like Christmas.

"It's cool in here," Will said, dismounting in the shade. He pulled his hands into the sleeves of his sweatshirt. "I mean like cold."

"It may feel cool now," Jed said, "but you'll be glad when the sun beats down on that meadow in the afternoon. I stayed here with Pete once after taking the trail crew out to their camp, and we liked it a lot."

"Well, let's set up camp, eat lunch, and explore," Mom said. "I think this is a wonderful place to spend the night."

Oriole curled up for a nap while we pitched our tents. The soft ground smelled of dirt and needles and old rotting wood. Mom, Allie, and I put our small duffels into our three-person tan dome tent and unrolled our sleeping bags while Jed and

Will rustled around in their tent. I took Red's horse blanket off his back and put it on a log to dry in the sun. It would serve as a soft warm bed for Oriole later.

"I don't know about you guys, but I'm going to explore that meadow," I said. "There's still time before lunch."

We made sure our animals were secure and safe on a "highline" before we walked up the trail to the meadow. The meadow spread out on a hill above us and rose higher and higher under a deep blue sky. Wildflowers burst through the grass, spreading splotches of color like paint from an artist's palette. The Big River Trail cut through the hillside below us and disappeared around a bend. Below the trail, the Middle Fork River glistened in the sun as it wound its way past the rising mountains on the other side. Will sat facing the river among the flowers. He pulled his sketch pad from his pack and started drawing. His map was growing.

The sun shone high above us. I felt its heat on my face and bare arms. Sweat beaded on my skin. Jed, Allie, and I walked slowly, trying to identify the yellow, blue, pink, and purple wildflowers and the tall grasses. All I recognized were dandelions—weeds—and they're not even from America. They were brought in from Europe.

Mom had taken botany classes in college, which means she studied plants. She loved identifying plants and helped us with some. We saw purple asters, bright yellow arnica, small white bistort, and many others. "Be careful not to pick any," she said. "They're native flowers and should be left alone to seed."

Will set his drawing aside. "Oh shoot. I was going to give Allie a 'boo-kay.' Now she'll have to settle for a look-see."

Mom laughed and walked down to where the Big River Trail cut across the meadow. She put on leather gloves and pulled a purple flower with a spiked top right out of the ground. I was shocked. Hadn't she just told us not to pick any flowers?

She held it high for us to see. "This pretty little plant is a Canada thistle, and although it looks nice, it isn't native to this meadow. It's considered a weed here. If you look around, you'll see lots of these near the trail. In the wilderness, feed for horses and mules must be free of weeds, but they're still brought in. Birds may have dropped some of the seeds, and they grew into plants. But probably seeds clung to horses, mules, or people and fell off here. If left here, weeds might compete with the native plants for space and water and choke them out. Some even have a kind of poison that kills other plants around them. This meadow could become a weed patch. That's why I didn't feel bad pulling this plant."

Allie put on her leather gloves and helped Mom pull the prickly thistles. Mom stuffed hers into a garbage bag she had brought but Allie held on to a few. "You know, these may be weeds, but they're still pretty. They'll make a nice centerpiece for our camp table. Might as well make use of 'em."

That night as we ate dinner cooked over a small camp stove and told tales of other campouts, we admired Allie's bouquet. She was right—the thistles were very pretty. Mom said we needed to take our full bag of weeds out with us when we left the campsite. Like dandelions, the wind blows thistle seeds and scatters them. Although these plants hadn't turned to seed yet, she didn't want even the smallest possibility that they might spread there.

The next morning we hiked to where Cox Creek meets the Big River Trail. A small spot next to the shallow creek had a couple logs where we sat and listened to the water. I tossed a few sticks to the other side of the narrow creek. Oriole splashed through the water and retrieved them. We laughed as she tossed one in the air, flipped around, grabbed it as it bounced off the ground, and raced back to us.

Suddenly Oriole dropped the stick and stared back up the trail. Her hackles went up along her back like a long thin ridge and she whined.

Someone was riding toward us. "Quiet, Oriole," I said. "We don't want to scare this person."

A tall horseman with a tall horse and mule rode down the trail. My heart pounded as he neared us. I was sure this was the lone horseman we had seen before.

Jed stood up when the man reached us. "Howdy, mister," Jed said. "Beautiful day, huh?"

The man stopped his chestnut brown horse, which pranced as if wanting to keep going. His sleek black mule stopped and put its head down to reach for a low shrub to nibble on. "Sure is," the man said.

The man was well over six feet tall. He looked about 50, was thin, and wore an old faded blue cowboy shirt and jeans, old beat up boots, and a dark brown cowboy hat that nearly hid his dark eyes. They seemed to pierce right through me. When he stared at Oriole, I grabbed her collar. She didn't bark or act like she would go after him, but I wanted the man to know she wasn't a threat.

Jed reached up and stuck out his hand for the man to grasp. "I'm Jed Scott. This is my mom, Kate, and my sister, Jessie. And these are Jessie's friends, Will and Allie. My dad's the ranger at Schafer Meadows."

The man stared a moment at Jed before shaking his hand. "Ben Morris."

"That's a beautiful mule you have, Mr. Morris," Mom said smiling.

The man didn't smile back. "Thanks, and the name's Ben."

Mom stopped smiling. "And I'm Kate."

"Where ya headed, Mr. Morris?" I asked.

"Upriver."

"Were you near Schafer Meadows recently? I thought I saw you heading the other direction not too long ago."

Mr. Morris's penetrating eyes turned in my direction. "Yep. I went out of the wilderness and came right back in."

"Well, stop in at Schafer if you go by again," Mom said. "We've always got a pot of coffee on."

"Well, thanks." Mr. Morris lightly kicked his horse. "I'll be going."

He looked over his shoulder as if to make sure his mule was still carrying an even load on its back. The packs looked pretty light for a mule that size.

When he was out of sight, Mom said, "Well, he's sure not the talkative type."

"He's kind of spooky-looking, if you ask me," I said. "Did you see how he stared at everyone? And he never smiled."

"Maybe he's just shy," Mom said. "Don't judge him too harshly."

"But why do you think he moves around so much?"

"Who knows? Maybe he's just enjoying the wilderness. People go on trips all over the place back here."

"Yeah, but usually they travel with other people."

"Not everyone. Some people like to travel alone. Look at Lost—he does it all the time."

"Well, I bet Mr. Morris is doing something he doesn't want to talk about."

"Oh, Jessie," Jed said. He sat back down on the log and patted Oriole, who leaned against his knee. "Give the guy a break. You think you're a big detective now because you solved a mystery at Schafer Meadows not long ago."

I felt my cheeks go red. "No I don't! I just think he's creepy, that's all."

"Yeah, I do, too," Allie said. "But I guess we should take your mom's advice and not judge him—at least not until we know differently."

"Okay," I said, "but I think we should pay attention to him if we keep seeing him around."

"Well, let's pay attention to getting packed up and back to Schafer," Mom said. "I'd like to make it in time for dinner."

SEVEN

Mother Bear

The three of us explored the long wet meadow on the other side of the airstrip at Schafer Meadows late the next morning. Will's dad, Don, had returned to Schafer with Game Warden Carlos and Pete while we were at Cox Creek on our overnight.

Thick willows and other brushy plants hid the water in places. We couldn't walk through there without soaking our feet, so we walked along the edge by the woods. Allie threw a stick for Oriole.

Oriole had found some deep holes to swim in, but she had also found some knee-deep mud, and it looked like she wore brown leggings. Allie's stick landed in a spot where Oriole wouldn't have to walk through mud when she got out. I was glad. It was too far to walk to the river, and I didn't want to have to hose her off later.

"How long do you think you and Allie can stay?" I asked Will.

"I don't know," Will said. "Dad said he'd call Allie's parents on the satellite phone after he and Carlos look for the lost bear cub's mother. They're taking Casey with them."

"Oh, I hope my parents will let me stay a while," Allie said. "I'm having too much fun. It's way better than babysitting my little brother. Too bad Casey has to work again instead of playing with Oriole."

"Hey, Will," I said. "Why don't we go to the horse camp to see if your dad and Warden Carlos found the mother bear?"

Will shook his head. "I don't think that's such a good idea. Dad doesn't like having kids around when he's working.

He says it's too distracting. And I bet Carlos wouldn't want us there, either."

Allie frowned. "Will's right. We don't want to make them mad and send us home. I really want to stay here longer."

"Well, okay," I said. "I was just trying to figure out something to do. Want to go to the river? We can walk the Schafer Creek Trail on the other side for a while, see what's over there."

We carried small daypacks with sandals made for walking in water. When we reached the river, we traded our hiking boots for the sandals and waded in the water. After the initial shock, the frigid water felt refreshing. The day was already getting hot. Oriole contented herself with swimming in tight circles and waiting for someone to throw her a stick.

Allie stood in the middle of the river and leaned over with her face close to the water. She held her long black hair back with one hand and pointed with the other. "Hey, look at the size of that fish!"

Will and I plunged through thigh-deep water to where she stood.

"Where?" Will asked as he leaned over.

"There!" Allie cupped both hands and splashed Will and me in the face.

That started a huge water fight. We chased each other around, scooping water and soaking whoever happened to be closest. We whooped and hollered.

Oriole barked, wanting to be part of the action. I tossed water high in the air in her direction. As the droplets fell she leaped at them, snapping and biting at the beads of water before landing with a huge splash. When it got too deep, Oriole swam, reaching out with her front paws and smacking the water, splashing herself. She learned that slapping the water with her paws made it go straight into the air and she could bite at it without anyone having to toss the water for her.

Oriole swam in small clumsy-looking circles, biting at water she slapped into the air by herself. We kids watched her and laughed hysterically.

We finally quit. Will's sandy hair hung limply on his forehead, dripping water into his eyes. Allie's hair drooped down her back. Her water-soaked glasses hung off one ear. We stood panting, laughing, and shivering in the water.

"Let's go to the other side and walk the trail to dry off," I said. "When we get hot, we can come back and drown each other again."

A short distance from the river the trail took off up a bank and into the woods. Already I felt the sun drying me. I was glad we had put our boots and socks into small plastic bags in our backpacks before wading the river. It was good to have dry feet as we hiked up the trail.

Oriole ran ahead, sniffing along the way. We hadn't even walked half a mile when we reached another trail that went left.

"Wonder where that goes?" Allie said.

"I think it goes up Dolly Varden Creek," I said.

"Dolly Varden Creek? Like the trout? Sounds like a great place to cast a line."

"If you want, we can come back here sometime."

Suddenly a thunderous WHOOSH filled the woods. All three of us jumped. I got ready to bolt when a loud *crock, crock* sounded overhead. Five ravens had flown from the trees, causing the commotion. They circled low above us. Three others sat in trees, staring down at us. We kids looked at each other and laughed nervously. I slowly let go of a breath I didn't know I'd been holding.

Will watched the ravens. "Uh-oh. That doesn't look good."

"Why, what's wrong with ravens?" Allie asked. "I think they're really cool birds."

"I do, too," Will said. "But usually if they hang out in an area, it means there's something dead nearby. We'd better keep our eyes open for bears."

"Hey, where's Oriole?" I asked.

Normally Oriole stays within sight, but she was nowhere to be seen. We hollered for her, but she didn't come.

"Do you think she took the other trail?" Will asked.

"I don't know." It wasn't like Oriole to wander off.

Suddenly, she appeared from the woods next to the trail leading up Dolly Varden Creek.

"Oh, Oriole," I said. "What were you doing? Don't go off like that again. You had me worried."

I bent down to hug her and drew back from a stench. "Whoa! What's that smell?"

I sniffed close to her back. "Oh, gag, Oriole! You stink!"

She had rolled in something that really reeked.

"Gross!" Allie said, turning green when the smell hit her. She held her nose.

"Do you always get so squeamish?" I asked.

"Only when I see or smell something rotten or dead."

"Let's see if Oriole will take us back to whatever she found," Will said. "We might want to move it farther away from the trail if it's close. Sometimes bears eat dead animals, and we don't want someone stumbling on a feeding bear. Dad says they can be really dangerous when they're guarding food."

"Yeah," Allie said. "Just like I feel when somebody tries to grab my dessert. Look out."

"Do you think it's okay for us to look for the animal or whatever it is?" I asked. "Seems it'd be dangerous for us, too."

"I think we'll be all right if we make a lot of noise first," Will said. "That way, if there is a bear in the area, it'll hear us coming and have time to leave. Besides, Oriole was there already, so I'm pretty sure there's no bear around. It probably would have chased her away."

We made noise—lots of it. My heart still hadn't completely stopped pounding after the scare from the ravens. We hooted and whistled and after a few minutes of making the loudest racket possible we followed Oriole back into the woods. A little off the trail, Oriole turned, looked back at us, and sat down. What we saw stopped us in our tracks.

"A bear!" whispered Allie.

It was a bear all right, but not feeding as we expected. An adult black bear lay on its side, dead. An arrow pierced its chest. Its stomach was bloated. All four legs were straight out and the paws were gone. On the ground was a dried pool of blood. Like the dead deer we'd found, the bear's eyes stared at nothing. Its tongue hung out of its mouth. Dirt coated the tongue where it touched the ground. Flies buzzed and hovered over the body. Oriole looked proud as she sat next to it.

"I think we found the cub's mother," Will said sadly.

Allie started to cry. "Why would someone do this to a bear?"

"Most of the time it's for their claws or hide. Or their head. But it looks like all they wanted were the claws this time."

"Why wouldn't they take the hide, too?"

"I don't know."

My eyes suddenly filled with tears. "Why would they want the claws?"

Will's brown eyes turned hard. "For money. Dad says there's big money in selling bear claws. People like to wear them as necklaces, use them for key chains, stuff like that."

Allie no longer looked green. She was red. "You mean someone would kill a bear just for its claws? Just for money? What kind of person does that?"

"Someone who has no respect for animals. Someone who doesn't care."

I felt red, too. "Boy that really makes me mad! Not only did they kill this bear, but whoever did this left a cub without its mother. What's going to happen to it? I don't see how the cub can survive alone. It's so tiny."

"You're probably right," Will said. "Whoever did this took two lives instead of one."

I felt incredibly sad. I wondered what it would be like to lose one of my parents. "Do you think the cub can be saved? Will Carlos and your dad try to rescue it?"

"Yeah. Sure. They'll set a small trap close by the mother, hoping to catch the cub. If they do they'll take it to a Fish, Wildlife and Parks rehabilitation center in Helena, Montana. It's kinda hard to get the cub out of the wilderness, though, because there aren't any roads back here. They'll have to fly it from Schafer to Helena."

Even though the bear reeked, I ran my hand along its side. She deserved to have someone care for her even though she couldn't feel it. Her sleek black fur felt rough and wiry. My hand didn't stink when I smelled it. "What'll they do at the rehab center, Will?"

"It's pretty cool. They'll raise the cub through the fall. Then they'll make a den for it like its mom would have done and return it to the wild in the winter when it's sleeping. When it wakes in the spring it'll be on its own but able to take care of itself without its mother."

"Whew," Allie said. "That makes me feel better. I always thought animals caught in the wild had to go to a zoo."

"Some do, especially grown animals. If an organization like the Helena rehab center can take it, it might have a chance to remain wild. If not, it might get sent to a zoo. But sometimes zoos won't take animals because they don't have enough room, so they have to be killed."

Allie's clenched hands flew to her face. "Oh, that's horrible! That's so unfair."

"You're not kidding," I said. "No matter what happens those animals lose. Some lose their babies forever. Some won't be returned to the wild, and if they aren't killed, they lose their freedom and spend their life in a cage at a zoo. What kind of life is that?"

Oriole padded away from the bear and sat next to me. I looked into her happy-looking eyes and felt glad that I had taken such good care of her in her young life. What would have happened if Dad hadn't saved her from the animal shelter? No matter how hard they try, not all shelters can keep all the animals that end up there. Some get euthanized, or as some people say, "put to sleep." Oriole might have lost more than her freedom—she might have lost her life.

"Well, here we go again," Will said. "We'd better go get my dad and Carlos. I doubt they'll care if we interrupt them now."

EIGHT

Coyote and Tracy Return

After we talked with Don and Warden Carlos at the horse camp, we kids went to the campground. I wanted to get away from the horror of the dead bear and visit with Jim. When I'm sad he always makes me feel good. I thought he might make Will and Allie feel better right now, too.

We found Jim kneeling next to his tent, removing the stakes. The tent collapsed to the ground and my heart sank with it.

"Are you leaving already, Jim?" I asked.

"Yep. It's time I left this campground to other people."

"But you just got here a few days ago. Can't you stay?"

"Nope."

Jim lifted the tent from the ground and grinned. "But if you pick your face up off the ground, you can help me carry my tent back to the plane before I take my gear to the cookhouse."

"What? Really? You're going to stay there? How'd that happen?"

"Fish and Game hired me to fly Game Warden Carlos in here earlier, and Carlos thinks he may need a pilot periodically until this poaching issue is resolved. Because I come to visit Charlie so often, I offered to help out at Schafer for free instead of standing around waiting for Carlos to need my services as a pilot. I'm now an official U.S. Forest Service volunteer. Your dad said I should move out of the campground and into the room next to Charlie upstairs in the cookhouse. We'll see how long that lasts. If Charlie snores too loudly, he may have to move out."

We all laughed. I felt better already.

We helped Jim roll up his tent and take it to his plane. We got to the cookhouse in time to see the two backpackers, Steve and Emma, go inside. I could tell it was them by Emma's bright red hair. Steve was showing Charlie his ankle when we came inside. The huge blister had healed so well in the past couple of days that he barely limped.

"Looks like it's probably healed enough that you can continue on your backpacking trip," Charlie said, "but you'd better take it easy for a few days."

"Yeah. I'm hoping our buddies Coyote and Tracy will return soon with some new boots for me. I gave them my boot size and drew around my feet on a piece of paper so they could try to get me a good fit."

"You know, even if they fit you perfectly, you'll need to break them in before going on a long trip. Most new boots are pretty stiff at first. You don't want to end up with more blisters."

"That's what Tracy said. She was hoping to find a pair that didn't take a lot of breaking in. We'll see what she comes up with."

"When do you expect your friends back?" Charlie asked.

Emma looked out the door. "We're hoping it'll be sometime today. If Coyote didn't have problems meeting the guy he had to see, that is."

Charlie sat at the table and whittled on a small duck. Wood chips flew across the table and into his lap. His hands swept them to the floor. "How long have you all known each other?"

"We met in college," Steve said. "We've been friends for about a year."

I wondered how close the four backpackers were as

friends. The night we visited them in the campground, Steve didn't look too happy with Coyote when Coyote turned down Cody's offer to use the Schafer Meadows first aid kit for Steve's blistered ankle. Steve didn't stick up for himself at the time. I didn't want to ask him any questions, though, because Emma was Coyote's girlfriend. It just didn't seem right to talk about her boyfriend behind her back. Steve, Tracy, and Emma were nice, but I wasn't sure about Coyote. He seemed to be calling all the shots. I thought he was pretty bossy.

"Well whaddya know. I think that's them walking up the trail by the airstrip," Emma said. She ran out the door. "C'mon, Steve. Let's go meet 'em."

Oriole seemed to think that was her clue to leave, too, and she slipped out the door before I could call her back. We went after her. She had run up to Coyote and Tracy for pats.

"Sorry," I said when we reached the others. "I try not to let my dog bother people."

Tracy took off her heavy-looking backpack and bent down to pat Oriole. She stepped on her long skirt when she tried to stand up and tripped. She laughed at herself. "No problem. We love dogs. She can visit anytime."

"How'd business go?" Emma asked.

"Good. In fact, great!" Coyote said. "The guy was really pleased with our products and thought progress is going well. He wants us to keep in touch."

Tracy looked down at Steve's feet. "Well, you look way better. We found a pair of hiking boots that oughta work for you if they fit right. The man at the store said they shouldn't need much breaking in, and they should give you good support."

Steve looked relieved. "Good. I was afraid I might have to cut my trip short."

"No way," Coyote said. "We're all in this together. If one goes, we all go."

Tracy took out a new pair of boots from her backpack and handed them to Steve. "Here. Try these."

Steve stepped out of his sandals and sat on the ground. He pulled up his socks, put the boots on, and walked a few steps. "They feel okay. They're sure better than those old shoes I've been wearing. My ankle feels pretty good right now. Let me walk around in them today to see if they'll work."

Coyote started walking toward the campground. "Let's hope so. We need to get going if we want to explore some more."

Tracy shrugged into her backpack and followed Coyote. "Let's give those boots a workout, Steve. Come on to the campground. I want to drop this pack."

The four walked off together, talking and laughing. Oriole watched them for a moment before trotting back to the cookhouse with us.

I glanced back at the group. "You know, when I'm in college I hope I can find a job during the school year that lets me take the summer off like they can. They're lucky to be able to go backpacking all summer."

Will stared after the four, too. "Yeah, must be nice. Look, Charlie's coming."

"Uh-oh. Could be bad news."

"Why do you say that?"

"'Cause I'm afraid he'll say your dad called on the radio and you have to go home."

"Nah. I think if my dad thought we might be in danger because of poachers in the area we'd have been long gone by now. Hi, Charlie," Will said.

Charlie met us with a smile. "Sure sounds like you three kids have been having your share of bad luck finding poached animals."

I stared at the short-cropped grass on the airstrip, waiting for Charlie's bad news. I was afraid to look him in the eye.

"Yeah, we haven't had much fun to ourselves." I glanced up quickly. "Except for the camping trips, of course. And visiting with you and Jim."

"Well, both your fathers and Kate have been feeling bad that your time together has been spoiled because of poachers and they want to do something about it."

"Like what?" I asked.

"How'd the three of you like to go visit the trail crew? Pete and Jed packed them in to one of the cabins for their next hitch. Your dad wants to go tomorrow and get them started on a new project. He thought you three might like to tag along with him."

"Oh, wow! That's great. Thanks, Charlie! Hey, you guys. We'd better go pack our bags. C'mon, Oriole. We gotta pack your food and bowl, too. Looks like fun's finally on its way!"

NINE

Gooseberry Cabin

The next morning dawned crisp and clear. Will, Allie, and I rode our horses in front of Dad, who led our mule, Kitty, behind him. Kitty carried a light load of camping gear and a change of clothes for us. Oriole romped ahead, calling an excited "Roooo!" Will wanted Casey to come with us, but Don needed him as a law dog to help investigate the dead bear incident.

At the campground, tents fell and poles and stakes clanged to the ground as the four backpackers took down their camp.

"Heading out today?" Dad asked.

Coyote stuffed stakes and tent poles into a green nylon sack. "Yep. Steve's feet have healed up and his new boots seem to be working okay."

"Where'd you decide to go?"

Coyote lashed his tent to the bottom of his backpack and jerked on the webbed straps that held the tent to the pack. He pulled harder on the webbing and grimaced. "We're not exactly sure. Just upriver somewhere. We'll talk more after we're on the trail."

"Well, have a safe trip. If Steve's feet bother him more, make sure he stops hiking and takes good care of them."

Coyote bent over and grabbed Emma's poles, shoving them into her stuff sack. "We'll do that. Thanks."

"Let's go," Dad said as he nudged Dillon, his buckskin, forward. "I want to get to Gooseberry Cabin before it gets too hot."

The Big River Trail passed Chair Mountain and Gable Peaks. We'd ridden past there on our overnight trip with Mom. I'd forgotten how beautiful the mountains were standing tall against the sky. We passed the meadow where Allie had collected the thistle weeds for a bouquet on our campout with Mom and Jed. And our trail went by the spot next to Cox Creek where we had met Ben Morris, the tall man with those piercing eyes and the big horse and mule.

"Where do you suppose Mr. Morris is right now?" I asked.

"Who knows?" Allie said. "It's been a few days since we saw him. He could be far away by now."

Our horses waded across Cox Creek in the cool dark forest. Soon the woods gave way to an open rocky slope where the sun warmed us. The trail hugged the bank of the Middle Fork River as we crossed another stream. We could see upriver for quite a distance.

"Winter Creek," Dad said. "We're making pretty good time."

We stopped for lunch under a group of lodgepole pine trees so the animals could have some shade. Some side trails wandered farther into the forest.

"Where do those go?" Allie asked.

"There's an outfitter's camp nearby. They bring dudes on trips—people who pay an outfitter to guide them back here. Doesn't appear anyone's home, though. We'd hear bells clanging from around the mules' necks and probably see some folks out and about."

Will pulled a peanut butter and blackberry jam sandwich from his saddlebags. It had gotten soggy from riding against his water bottle. He didn't seem to notice as he scraped his finger against the side of the sandwich bag and sucked the jam off his finger. "We've been pretty lucky having the trail to ourselves. I like that."

"Well, enjoy the solitude, because there won't be much once we get to Gooseberry Cabin and hook up with the trail crew. It gets pretty noisy in the little cabin with everyone talking and banging around making meals and stuff."

Will chomped into his sandwich. "That's okay. That's noise I like."

We settled into eating lunch. The river rippled gently past us. Oriole took a dip in the river and shook off all over Dad when she got out. She has a way of finding someone to soak, and it was Dad's turn. He saw her coming but couldn't get up fast enough. He banged his head on a low-hanging tree branch. His sage green Forest Service shirt and pants were riddled with water drops. He wiped his face with his Smokey Bear bandana.

"Come here, you no count hound," Dad said, holding his sore head.

Oriole wagged her tail and leaned against him, soaking his pant leg more. Fortunately for her, all Dad could do was laugh. "My fault," he said, backing away from her. "Here, take these and go away."

Dad gave Oriole a couple of dog treats to eat while we finished our lunch. Then she stretched out in the sun for a nap. Small twigs, leaves, and blades of grass clung to her wet coat. I ruffled her fur to clean her off before we left.

We finally arrived at Gooseberry Cabin by late afternoon, hot and sweaty. Saddle sore, I had walked Red for a couple of miles, but I was still stiff and sore after a long day on horseback. I tied Red to a post next to the small cabin's wooden porch.

The one-room log cabin was painted the same dark brown I was used to seeing in the wilderness. An overhanging roof covered the porch. The back of the cabin had no window, but the two sides each had one. Without them, I was sure the cabin would be dark inside.

We untied the manty packs from Kitty and dropped them onto the porch. Dad wriggled loose four large L-shaped bolts attached to a metal door on the cabin. He wrestled the heavy door off the hinges, slid it along the porch, and leaned it against the cabin wall. Another wooden door stood inside with a lock on it.

I put my hand on the metal door. It had a wooden backing. "Why two doors? And why one with metal?"

Dad jiggled his Forest Service key in the lock and swung the inside door open.

"It's to keep bears out. Crews who stay in these backcountry cabins know they need to store their food well and keep the cabins clean so they don't attract bears, but they're not always successful. Bears, especially grizzlies, have incredible strength. They've been known to rip doors off their hinges or push them in, and they've had many a free lunch once inside a cabin."

He pointed to one of the bolts on the outside cabin wall. "We keep the metal outer door off the cabin when the crews are here but lock the cabin tight when they're gone for the day. The outer door can discourage a bear from trying to break in."

"I bet it can," Allie said. "A bear'd have a hard time pulling it off. Have bears tried to get into this cabin?"

"They've tried their luck a time or two." Dad shut the inner door. "Come on. Let me show you something before we go inside. Bring your horses on around."

He led us to a small wooden post corral close to the cabin. Both ends of the corral stopped at the side of a brownish-red wooden barn about the size of a large closet. The outside had dirt smeared all over it. We tied our animals to corral rails and removed their saddles, bridles, and blankets. Dad opened the barn door. Stacked hay and grain bins filled the little building. We tossed out some hay, grabbed curry combs, and began brushing down our horses.

Dad chuckled. "You kids sure don't observe much."

I glanced around. So did Will and Allie.

"What do you mean, Dad?"

"Look closely at the sides of this barn. What do you see?"

"Just a bunch of dirty—Whoa! Look at that!"

I hurried to one side of the barn and placed my hand flat against it. Underneath my palm was a distinct print from a bear's paw, and where my spread fingers touched were claw marks. What I had thought was dirt on the building were actually bear paw prints—lots of them. Sometime after a rain that turned the ground muddy, a bear had scratched or pawed the side of the building. It was probably trying to get inside. There were so many prints they practically covered the entire barn.

Will walked around looking at the prints, shaking his head. "This is crazy! That bear really wanted to get into the barn. Do you know how it happened?"

We put our curry combs away and Dad closed the barn door and locked it. "One spring when the trail crew came to the cabin, they found the barn door ripped off its hinges. A 50-gallon drum used to hold grain had been rolled outside and down toward the river. Its top had been peeled back like a tin can, and all the grain was gone. One look at the drum and the sides of the barn told the crew that a bear had stolen the feed. A sack of alfalfa pellets stored in the barn was also gone. The bear was hungry enough or determined enough to take the time to find a way inside. It obviously got what it wanted. It took our crew some time to fix the door, but we think the barn is now more bear proof."

Allie ran her fingers along some deep scratch marks in the wood. "It's sure a good thing it didn't try for the cabin instead."

Dad nodded. "Right. Now you know why the cabin has the extra door. So far, so good. Let's take our things inside the cabin. The trail crew ought to be back soon. Maybe we can have dinner ready for them."

Back at the cabin, Dad and Will tossed their sleeping
bags into the small loft over the porch and carried their duffels
with clothes and gear up the wooden ladder. Allie and I rolled
out our bags on bunks by the door. I had brought Red's saddle
blanket inside for Oriole. It didn't take long for her to curl up
and fall sound asleep.

"Okay," Dad said. "Ready to be backcountry chefs? This
is a super easy meal to make."

Will peeled and sliced potatoes while Allie cut up carrots
for dinner. I munched on some of the cut carrots until Allie
slapped my hand away. I tried to watch Dad make hamburger
patties but tears swam in my eyes from slicing onions and I
couldn't see.

Will set his knife and potato peeler on the table and
rubbed his hands together. "So now what do we do?"

"You tell 'em, Jessie," Dad said. "I'm going outside to
make a fire for our dinner."

"Okay," I said. "We all get our own meal wrapped in alu-
minum foil. So, spread out some foil on the table. Heap a layer
of veggies onto the foil, put a hamburger patty on top, and then
another layer of veggies on top of the burger."

The small cabin smelled of raw burger and veggies as we
filled each foil square. We tightly wrapped the foil around each
dinner, pinching the edges to seal in the juices. Allie carried a
large platter with the burger meals outside to Dad's fire. Dad
put the foil packs under the red hot coals to cook. I couldn't
wait to eat. It was one of my favorite camping dinners.

While the food cooked and Oriole slept, we kids explored
outside. Celie, Mandy, and Cody had pitched their tents close
to the cabin, even though they had settled into the cabin a few
days ago. Dad had radioed them that we were coming and the
crew gave us their bunks for the night.

"Do you think the trail crew thinks we're afraid to sleep outside?" Allie asked.

Will shook his head. "Nah. I think they like us and want to make us feel at home."

"I think so, too," I said. "It's a great gift. Enjoy it."

Gooseberry Cabin faces the Middle Fork River. We reached it by wobbling and stumbling over rounded river rocks of red and green on a wide gravel bar. The clear water felt cold against our skin as we waded toward the other side. From there, the cabin looked tiny. High rolling mountains to the west and tall spruce and fir trees surrounded us as the immenseness of the wilderness engulfed us. I felt like an ant.

When we returned we found Dad still stoking the fire to keep the coals alive. His stick poked a small log nearly turned to ashes. "There's one important thing you guys need to know. The outhouse is up the hill behind the cabin."

"Oh, good," Will said. "I was about to ask that."

"There's a great story behind that outhouse," Dad said.

A great story about an outhouse? Dad's losing it, I thought, but I kept quiet.

Dad grabbed two strong sticks and picked up a sizzling foil package between them. He turned the foil over, scraped out a small place for it with the sticks, and buried it beneath more coals.

"A number of years ago when the old outhouse needed to be replaced, someone thought the new one should go on the slope behind the cabin. The view of the mountains is great, and there's plenty of privacy because it's surrounded by trees. This outhouse is different from most others because the builders decided not to put walls up. All you'll see up there is a short square wooden platform with a hole in the middle. You can commune with nature while you sit."

Dad's grin told me he was really enjoying himself.

"Eeewww," I said. "You mean it's open to the air? Doesn't sound like it'd be fun when it's raining or windy."

"Yeah, but you can watch the stars at night and feel the sun on your face on a warm day."

"Not to mention flies. It must draw them."

"I 'spose so, but other outhouses do, too. But the story doesn't end there. Once a packer brought his young daughter to Gooseberry. When she needed to go, his daughter asked him where the outhouse was. He directed her up the hill. A little while later, the girl came back into the cabin. 'Daddy, that's not an outhouse,' she said. 'It's just an 'out'.'"

We all roared with laughter. Will ran toward the back of the cabin.

"Where ya goin'?" Allie shouted.

"To check out the Out!"

TEN

Visitors

The trail crew arrived at the cabin just as Dad was taking the wrapped foil dinners out of the coals. Celie, Mandy, and Cody had dust all over their faces and clothes. They dropped leather work gloves on the porch and hung hardhats on nails. Dried sweat caked their foreheads and matted their hair.

Mandy set her daypack down outside the door. She wiped her face with a dirty bandana and took a deep breath. "I'm beat. But mmmmm! Whatever's cooking smells great!"

The aroma of roasted onions, potatoes, and cooked hamburger filled Gooseberry Cabin as Dad set the steaming, crackling foil packages on the table. Oriole stood next to him with her nose in the air, sniffing and wagging her tail.

One luxury of Gooseberry Cabin is running water, fed from a spring and filtered for drinking water. The crew washed up and everyone grabbed a fork and a foil dinner. We went outside to eat on the porch and enjoy the evening.

"Where's Lost?" I asked. "We made a dinner for him, too."

Cody put his plate on his lap, unwrapped his foil, and forked a hunk of burger and sliced potato. "Oh, he decided to go off on another backpack trip. I expect him back in a day or so."

Celie stabbed a forkful of onions and carrots. She cupped her free hand under her chin to catch the vegetables that threatened to fall. "We should place bets on whether he makes it back. That poor guy ought to carry a GPS with him—you know, like some people have in their car to help them find their way around cities and stuff. He could set a point on it when he leaves someplace so he can at least get back again if he gets lost."

Cody leaned against the cabin, stretching his dusty legs in front of him. He blew on his burger and took another bite. "Yeah, he probably should, but lots of GPS units don't work in the wilderness any more than a cell phone. The mountains block the signal in deep canyons. And I'm not too sure Lost would want one anyway. Sometimes I think he enjoys all the adventures he has trying to find his way around places."

Celie shrugged. "Someday his luck may run out."

Dad lifted his fork and pointed it at the trail behind the cabin. "Well, look who's here."

I stood up. "Is it Lost?"

In the distance the heads of four backpackers bobbed toward us. Coyote led the way, walking quickly, with Emma, Tracy, and Steve trudging slowly behind him.

Coyote turned around and walked backwards, spreading his arms wide. "C'mon, step on it!" he hollered. "I want to set up camp before dark."

Oriole started barking and ran toward the trail. Coyote saw us about that time and stopped. "Oh. Didn't know anyone would be at the cabin. Sorry to intrude—again."

Dad set his plate on the porch. "No problem. You've had a long day, especially coming here on foot. Where are you headed?"

Oriole leaned against Emma, and Emma scratched her on the head. "We planned to stay on Clack Creek across the river. You told us at Schafer about a campsite not too far up the trail, but we didn't think it would take this long to get there."

"Right, there's a campsite, but you've got another couple miles to go before you get there."

Steve's shoulders drooped. "I don't think I can go another mile. These new boots haven't given me any grief, but, man, I don't have any energy left."

Tracy grabbed her pack straps and shifted the weight from her shoulders. "Steve's right. We're all beat. Maybe there's a place closer by where we can stay the night and then head out early tomorrow morning."

Dad pointed upriver to where Gooseberry Cabin's small meadow narrowed. "You're welcome to stay up there. There's plenty of room for your tents."

"You've had to deal with us enough as it is," Coyote said. "I don't like it."

"It's okay. We've had other parties stay there at times."

Emma stopped patting Oriole. "Look, Coyote, we can stay far enough from these folks to give them their space. The river's here so we'll have plenty of water. And we'll be in much better shape to go on tomorrow."

Tracy and Steve agreed. Coyote had no choice but to stay. "Okay. We leave first light tomorrow morning, though. Let's go."

Coyote led his small band away from us and closer to the river.

Mandy watched them go. "What a weird group. You'd think they'd come here to enjoy themselves, but that Coyote guy sure pushes them. I don't get it. He works them harder than you work us, Tom, and we're getting paid."

Dad just shook his head. "Hard saying why they stick together. Makes you wonder what they'll do when summer's over and they have to go back to school."

It made no sense to me that they'd stay together once they left the wilderness. I couldn't imagine why Emma hung around with Coyote. How could she be his girlfriend? She seemed pretty nice to me. So did Tracy and Steve. But Coyote seemed rude, pushy, and like he thought he was better than everyone else. Why didn't they just tell him not to boss them around anymore? They sure didn't act like friends.

Oriole came and sat next to me. I hugged her and gently pulled her ears. She closed her eyes and leaned into me.

Will and Allie roasted marshmallows over the fire for S'Mores. Allie shoved Will out of the way to get to the best spot. Will tried to shoulder her away but fell over backwards, feet in the air. The gooey burnt marshmallow toppled from the end of the stick and landed on Will's nose. The black mess was like pulled taffy as he took it off his nose, stuck out his tongue, and crammed it in his mouth. They laughed and joked with each other. It was easy to see they were friends. What a difference from the four backpackers! And I could tell Will and Allie liked me, too. We made a pretty cool group.

ELEVEN

Trail Work

Will led our mule Kitty, who carried big empty canvas packs as we hiked to meet the crew at the work site on the Bowl Creek Trail. The crew had stashed their tools in the woods so they didn't have to haul them back and forth every day to the same site. All we carried were our own daypacks.

Celie handed shovels to us kids. She gave Dad a pulaski. It had a small hoe on one end of the head to scrape the ground or pick out rocks and an axe on the other side to chop things like roots or small trees.

Being crew leader, Celie was in charge for the day. She paired Mandy, Allie, and me together as work partners and Dad with Will. Cody would be her partner. We'd all work as a team, but we kids would have a crew member to coach us.

Celie gathered everyone together for a safety lesson on how to use our tools. "I don't want to have to pack anybody out with an injury, so pay attention."

We listened closely. Then she gave us our jobs for the day. "Since we've got extra help today, we're going to try to finish the turnpike in this section."

Allie looked confused. "My family rode on a turnpike in the Midwest once. It was a toll road. We had to throw money into a bin every few miles or so. That's not what we're making, is it? A toll trail, I mean?"

Celie shook her head. "No. Some trails have places that are always wet or are in sensitive areas that can get damaged easily by horses and mules. We build what we call 'turnpike' to prevent that. Come here. I'll show you."

We walked a short distance up the trail to a gentle rise where trail dirt turned to gravel a couple of inches higher than the rest of the path. Logs lay lengthwise along either side of the trail, secured to the ground by heavy-duty wooden stakes. A black cloth lay on the ground between the logs the width of the footpath.

"This is called filter cloth. It allows water to seep downward but it can't come back up," Celie said. "And see where we've completed the turnpike? See what's on top of the filter cloth? Some places have rock, but we fill between the logs with enough packed gravel to make the turnpike smooth and even."

Celie walked on the gravel laid down between the logs. "When people ride this part of the trail, their animals have to pay attention where they walk so they don't fall off. They tend to stay on the turnpike—the lined path—and don't damage the ground around it."

"Cool idea," Will said. "I've seen these types of things before but never knew why they were put there."

We spent the day working on the short section of turnpike. Mandy, Allie, and I filled burlap bags with gravel we dug from a gravel bar along nearby Bowl Creek. Cody and Celie loaded the full bags onto the trail crew's horse and mule and our mule, Kitty. The animals hauled the heavy gravel to the work site where Dad and Will dumped bag after bag of gravel between the logs. We packed down and leveled the gravel on the turnpike and slowly worked our way to the end.

By the time we finished for the day, I could barely move. My shoulders and arms ached and my legs felt like lead. We had added about 20 feet to the turnpike, enough to finish it. That section of trail would stay dry in the future. At last the trail crew could move up Bowl Creek beyond that horrible spot. Even though I was so tired, it was great to see how much work we had all done.

Oriole had spent most of the day lounging like a queen in the shade next to the trail. Occasionally she went with Dad and Will to the creek to cool off or brought sticks for me to throw. But hiking the past couple of days must have meant she didn't get all of her beauty rest, because she slept a lot.

On the hike back to Gooseberry Cabin, Oriole was wide awake and wanted to play. I could barely put one foot in front of the other and just kicked sticks down the trail for her. She'd drop one at my feet, watch my face while she walked backwards facing me, and then snatch up the stick in her teeth when I kicked it weakly in the air for her.

Celie had hiked back to Gooseberry Cabin an hour before the rest of us. When we arrived, the smell of oil-fried tortillas and melted cheese drifted out the cabin door. My mouth started to water. Celie had set the table and fixed a dinner of our choice of chicken or cheese enchiladas. A large salad bowl sat in the center of the table, and a no-bake cheesecake with cherries on top waited on a counter. I don't think anything ever looked so good to me.

We washed up at the sink and staggered to the table. Cody and Mandy sat on one of the bunks because the table couldn't hold us all. Celie dished an enchilada for Dad and then held up two small bowls.

"Red or green?" she asked with a sly smile.

Dad sat back and put his elbows on the arms of his chair. He folded his fingers together and laughed. "Thanks. I'll take red."

Cody tried to look in the bowls that Celie held high in the air. "Red or green what? What does she mean?"

I held up my plate as Celie put an enchilada on it. "I'll take green. Where'd you learn that, Celie?"

From one bowl Celie spooned some red chili sauce onto Dad's enchilada and from the other she spread green sauce on mine.

"I have friends who live in northern New Mexico. They told me New Mexican cooking differs from Mexican by how the sauces are made. Mexicans use a tomato base, while New Mexican sauces are made from red or green chilies. They also said red chilies are almost always hotter than green— sometimes a lot hotter."

"That's right," Dad said, cutting into his enchilada.

"My friends said when you go into a restaurant in New Mexico and order, the server asks if you want red or green."

"Yeah," I said. "And if you don't know the answer, people know you're not from around there."

Allie took the enchilada Celie offered her and looked at the two sauces. "What if you don't know which one you like? I'd hate to take the red one and burn my mouth, but maybe I wouldn't like the flavor of the green one."

"You can say you want a little 'Christmas,' which means both, to see which you like better."

"Okay, then I'd like a little Christmas, please."

Dinner was great, although it made me homesick for New Mexico and my best friends, June and Julie. Each day away from them got a bit easier, especially with Will and Allie around, but I still missed them terribly and wrote often. I hoped they were writing to me, but mail only comes to Schafer Meadows when Packer Brad brings it in on horseback or when someone hikes in and remembers to bring it from Spotted Bear. It takes a while to reach us. I really didn't know if June and Julie had written me. I'd probably find out when we got back.

After we washed the dinner dishes, we went outside to watch the mountains change from green to yellow to pink in the dusk. It seemed every muscle in my body ached, but it felt good. I had learned how hard the trail crew worked, but also that I could work with them and enjoy it.

"Can we help some other time?" I asked.

Dad put his arm around my shoulder. "You mean you didn't get enough today?"

"I never worked so hard in my life, but it was great."

"Hey," Cody said. "You guys can help whenever you want."

"Right," Mandy said, patting me on the back. "And you can be my partner anytime, Jessie."

The night sky didn't appear for a long time. I really wanted to watch the stars, but my eyes kept closing. Oriole slept soundly at my feet. Will and Allie had already gone in to bed by the time I called Oriole to come inside with me. I fell into bed and must have fallen asleep immediately.

Before opening my eyes the next morning, I heard someone softly clumping around in the one-room cabin. Something metal clanked onto the table. The smell of coffee filled the room. I love the smell of coffee but not the taste, so I started to drift off to sleep again. But the sound and smell of bacon sizzling on the stove drew me back to the present. I love bacon!

Yawning and stretching, I sat up and watched Will whisk pancake batter in a large metal bowl. "You're up early, Will. Need some help?"

"Nah, I'm just getting stuff going. Your dad wanted to get an early start out of here so I thought I'd do breakfast."

I reached up, shoved my hands against the bedsprings of the upper bunk, and pushed hard. The bedsprings gave way easily. No one was up there.

"Where's Allie? When did she get up?"

"She's out at the corral helping your dad feed the horses and Kitty."

Oriole was nowhere in sight.

"Guess my dog deserted me, too, huh?"

"Yep. She's out making sure the trail crew gets up. She already went for a morning swim."

Oriole arrived then, drenched and happy, and stuck her cold wet head on my lap. I screeched and jumped out of bed before she could soak me, too.

"Wait a minute, Oriole. Before you decide to shake water all over the cabin, you go back outside." I made shooing motions with my hands. Oriole cocked her head at me. "You heard me. Git!"

Oriole trotted out the cabin door in the direction of the barn. I fixed her breakfast and set it outside on the porch, hoping she wouldn't try to come back inside until she had dried off. Will had politely stepped outside so I could dress. After I put on my riding jeans and a T-shirt, he came back inside. I stuffed my sleeping bag into its sack, put my dirty clothes into a small bag, and helped Will finish getting breakfast ready. He cooked pancakes on a flat iron grill on the stove. I set out plates and silverware and made coffee. In the backcountry, the cooks don't have to help with the dishes, which was okay with me. By the time the crew and Dad and Allie came in, breakfast was ready.

"I think we'll make headway on the trail today, Tom," Celie said to Dad as she grabbed a piece of bacon. "Getting that turnpike out of the way really helped a lot. We should probably get halfway to the top with any luck."

"Good. You're doing a great job. This trail is a tough one. It really helps to have an experienced crew who like each other. You work better that way. I've seen crews who fight and bicker about little things, and it makes working very hard at times."

Mandy pushed her plate away and moved a strand of bushy hair back into her loose ponytail. "How could we not like working here? We've got the best job in the whole world in the world's best place."

Dad grinned. "You keep thinking that, Mandy. You three sure make my job a lot easier."

When breakfast ended, I broke down and said I'd wash the dishes. The crew wanted to get going, and Dad and Allie were getting our horses saddled for the ride back to Schafer Meadows. Will had cooked breakfast, so that left me. I didn't mind, though. Having a sink and running water in the cabin really made things a lot easier than having to wash dishes in a big metal basin like we usually have to do.

Outside the open doorway, Oriole lay on the porch with her front paws crossed, gazing out toward the river. She looked like she owned Gooseberry Cabin and its surroundings.

I plowed into the hot soapy suds to wash a dish and held it in mid-air. "You know, Oriole, you could have helped me wash these dishes. I think you'd have enjoyed it. Of course, Dad would have had a fit."

Oriole's head turned. I looked at her black eye and chest.

Sometimes at home in New Mexico I'd sneak a plate for her to lick before it went into the dishwasher where the water's hot enough to kill germs. This time Oriole just looked at me like it was beneath her dignity to wash dishes. She put her head on her paws and shut her eyes.

I stood on the porch drying the last dish and watched Allie finish saddling her horse, Lily, at the corral. Dad had loaded Kitty, our mule, with garbage to take back to Schafer. All our animals stood tied inside the corral, quietly waiting for us.

Dad called everyone inside the cabin, closed the door, and pulled out the map. He asked Celie, Cody, and Mandy to sit around the table while he gave them last minute project instructions. He asked us kids to stay in case we had any thoughts from the day before. I was really happy that he did that. It meant he appreciated the work we'd done. Dad finally rose from the table, ready to start the long ride back to Schafer.

"Hello the camp!"

Cody looked up from the map on the table. "Did you guys hear someone calling us?"

We listened.

"Hello the camp!" someone called.

Will opened the cabin door. We watched Lost as he tried
to walk to the cabin from the direction of the river. He had
trouble getting to us because Oriole kept making tight circles
around him, weaving in and out of his legs. He couldn't make
much forward progress.

"Oriole, get back here," I said. "Lost isn't going anywhere."

Oriole ran back to the porch and turned to watch Lost.
She wagged her whole back end and stomped her front paws
eagerly. I held her by her collar.

"She really loves you, Lost. She only does that to her best
friends."

When Lost got to the cabin, he dropped his heavy pack
on the porch and reached out with one hand, slowly lowering
himself until he could sit. "Wow! What a trip!" he said.

"Looks like you had a rough one," Dad said.

"You could say that."

Lost's pant legs were soaked to the knees from having
forded the river. He wore sandals and had slung his boots over
his shoulders to keep them dry. His pants and T-shirt had dried
blood on them—lots of blood.

"What happened to you?" Cody asked. "You look like you
got mauled or something."

Lost put his hands on his chest, stared down at his bloody
clothes, and ran his hands to his waist. "Looks pretty bad,
doesn't it?"

Lost's Story

Lost dropped his boots on the porch and leaned against his pack. "Yesterday I was on my way back here from a lake way up in the mountains. I met some folks from Illinois. They had a dog with them—a shepherd cross named Max—and he wasn't used to hiking. His paws were too soft to walk that far and the pads had gotten so worn they started to bleed."

Mandy shook her head. "Oh wow. That must have hurt."

"Yeah. That dog was in a lot of pain. He limped pretty badly. Finally Max just stopped and lay down in the middle of the trail. He wouldn't move any farther. That's when I ran into them. The people didn't seem to know what to do with the dog. I had a first aid kit with me and told them I'd try to fix Max's paws so he could walk, but they needed to get him out of the wilderness and to a vet fast. We happened to be in a good spot to set up camp. I said I'd help them with Max if they would stay put for the night to give him a rest before taking him out.

"I had a bunch of gauze and adhesive tape and some salve in my first aid kit. We wrapped the dog's paws in enough gauze to cushion them from rocks, roots, or hard ground and taped them as well as we could. We put duct tape on top of the adhesive tape to try to give the bandages more strength."

Lost looked at each of us and laughed. "Max looked like he had silver booties on, like he was from Outer Space. The people were so grateful for my help they asked me to spend the night with them. I stayed because I wanted to make sure the dog was all right. They fed me dinner last night and breakfast this morning. When I left, the dog was walking pretty well. You'd never know he was hurt except he walked like he had heavy boots on."

"So how'd you get blood all over yourself?" Dad asked.

"We had to lay Max on his side to doctor his paws, and he didn't like it at first. I think it scared him to have so many people hovering around. He tried to get up, but I held him down by leaning on him and putting my arms on his legs. The others held Max from behind, but I had to be in front to put the salve and gauze on. He howled and thrashed about and got blood all over me. Lucky me, I was the only one."

"That's a lot of blood on you," I said.

"Well, Max was big and got really scared when we all grabbed at him and wouldn't let him up. You wouldn't believe the fight he put up. At least he wasn't a biter or I'd be wearing my own blood."

Lost had dark reddish brown showing underneath his fingernails. He must have had blood all over his hands and hadn't washed it all off.

"Do you have a change of clothes?" Dad asked.

"Yeah. I left some here at Gooseberry. The bloodstains won't come out of these clothes, but they're grubby hiking clothes anyway. I know it's not a good idea to wear bloody clothes in the wilderness because the smell might attract animals, and I didn't want some bear sniffing around me. But they were the only ones I had."

"Okay. So what are your plans? Will you stay here at Gooseberry with the crew?"

"For a while. Backpacking was great but it's really good to be here. The best part was I didn't get lost this time. 'Course I never left the Clack Creek Trail."

"You can't fool me, Lost," Cody chuckled. "Tell me the truth—did you ask those people which way it was to Gooseberry Cabin?"

Lost dropped his head to his chest. Only his eyes looked up at Cody. "So what? At least I got here."

Cody smacked his hands together. "Yes! I knew it!"

Dad grabbed his saddlebags. "One last question, Lost. Which way were the people with the dog headed?"

"They said something about going over Switchback Pass and then down to the Spotted Bear River and out to their car."

"Okay. I'll notify Spotted Bear to watch for them—just in case their dog has more problems."

"Fine, but I think they planned to take their time and let their dog's paws heal as much as possible. They didn't seem in any hurry to get out, even to go see a vet."

"Yeah, but who knows how long it will take Max's paws to heal if they keep moving? There may be a crew in the area that could check on them. I'd hate for their dog's paws to get infected, especially since they didn't seem to know what to do."

Will, Allie, and I followed Dad to the Gooseberry barn. Oriole raced ahead and slithered under the corral fence. She waited for us with a wagging tail.

"Can I ask you something, Dad?" I asked.

"Sure, Jessie. What is it?"

"You seemed like you didn't believe Lost. Do you think he made up that story?"

"No, not necessarily. It's just that he had a lot of blood on him. More than I would have expected from cut dog paws."

"But why wouldn't you believe him? He's Cody's friend."

"I know. Maybe I'm just a little too sensitive because of the poaching that's happening around here."

"You think he's the poacher?"

Dad untied his horse, Dillon, from the corral fence. "No. He doesn't seem like the type. I'm just being cautious. After all, we really don't know Lost that well. C'mon. Let's get moving. Mom and Charlie will probably have something ready for dinner when we get back to Schafer."

"You're thinking of dinner already?" I said. "Didn't you feed my dad, Will?"

Will punched my arm and smiled. "Hey! You can't blame me if he didn't eat. There was enough food for an army."

"Yeah," Allie said. "And you ate like you were the whole army. The rest of us are still starved."

"Okay, you three," Dad said. "Let's get those appetites on the trail. Lead the way, Oriole."

"Go ahead, Dad," I said. "I'll catch you in a minute."

With Red's reins in my hand I led him to the river so he could get a quick drink. It's neat listening to him suck water through puckered lips. I patted him on his shiny brown neck and took one last look at Gooseberry Cabin, snug against the mountains. A small leaf from a nearby willow fluttered to the ground at my feet. I leaned over to pick it up and dropped it into the Middle Fork River.

"See you at Schafer Meadows," I said as the leaf floated by.

THIRTEEN

To Catch a Poacher

It was like homecoming at Schafer. Mom, Jed, Charlie, Pete, Jim, Don, and Warden Carlos greeted us. Casey ran to meet Oriole when he saw her at the barn. The two dogs romped and played like they hadn't seen each other for years.

Jim took off his blue pilot's cap and motioned to us with it. "Hungry? C'mon to the cookhouse. I've got dinner ready and the table set."

Jim had gathered a bunch of daisies, put them into two vases, and set them on the kitchen table as centerpieces.

"Those look really beautiful, Jim," Allie said, as she scooted her chair close to her plate, awaiting the arrival of the food. "Where'd you find them?"

Jim grinned and glanced at Mom. "Down by the river. Thought they'd be a nice way to welcome you back home until Kate here told me that they're oxeye daisies, and they're a weed."

Allie stood up and brought a vase of daisies closer to get a better look. "No, really? Why is it that all the pretty plants around here are weeds? Why can't there be some that are native?"

"There are," Mom said, "but we don't pick them. Some, like certain orchids, are pretty sensitive to disturbance, and if you pick them, they may never grow back. Others are so beautiful that a lot of people pick them without realizing that other people are doing it, too, and after a while, there aren't any left. I told Jim he can pick all the oxeye daisies he wants, especially if he can get them by the roots so they won't grow back. They're pretty, but they take up the same space natives need, so we try to keep them out of the wilderness."

Allie set the vase back on the table. "Well, Jim, if you want more weeds for centerpieces, I'll be glad to help you find some Canada thistle. I'm good at that."

They both laughed and we settled in to eat.

Jed went to the stove and brought back a covered cast iron pot called a Dutch oven. We use them occasionally on back-country trips when we want to cook food slowly and have the time to feed charcoal to the oven to keep it going. Jed had to carry the heavy pot with both hands. He put it on the table and lifted the lid. Inside was the most wonderful looking lasagna I'd ever seen.

"Who baked this?" Warden Carlos asked. "I haven't seen anyone cook with a Dutch oven in a long time, and never lasagna."

Charlie asked for Mom's plate and began dishing out food with a spatula. "Jim did. He had all day to do it, so it was a perfect project for him. Give him something he has to hurry with and it'll never get done."

"Oh, give me a break, old man," Jim said. "I'll take you on anytime."

Charlie dished out some lasagna, passed it to Don, and shook the spatula at Jim. "You're just sore because I beat you in the last Backcountry Horsemen's cook-off when we competed against 20 other folks for the best chili recipe."

"Yeah, years ago when we worked together," Jim said, passing his plate. "But that was pure luck. I ran out of onions, or I'd have beaten you hands down."

Jed grabbed the plate Charlie handed him. "This looks like really good stuff. Tell you what. Why don't you two have another cook-off? I'd hate to see your talents go to waste. I'll gladly judge the contest."

"Me, too," Pete said, cutting into a piece of lasagna with his fork. He elbowed Jed. "But the way you eat, there probably wouldn't be enough for both of us to judge. Their talents wouldn't go to waste—just to your waist."

Dinner ended up being a typical Schafer meal after someone returns from a trip—great food, lots of fun conversation, and endless questions about what events took place, both on the trip and at the ranger station. While Charlie and Jed got the dish water ready, I let Oriole and Casey into the kitchen. They waggled their way around the room, hoping to get handouts. Casey scored a couple crumbs under the table, but Oriole got skunked. She looked expectantly at everyone, but no one paid any attention to her. She curled up in a corner with a sad look and a disappointed sigh.

"Better luck next time, girl," I said. "You gotta be quicker than Casey. He's a faster vacuum cleaner than you are. He could've been named Hoover."

After we washed the dishes, table talk turned to what Don and Warden Carlos had discovered in their investigation into the poached deer and bear.

Will slid into the long bench against one kitchen wall so he could sit by Don. "Hey, Dad, can you and Carlos tell us what you do to catch a poacher?"

Don scratched Casey behind one ear. "I'll let Carlos tell you. It's his job, not mine."

"True," Carlos said, "but without help from Forest Service law enforcement officers like your dad here, my work would be much tougher. We game wardens are spread pretty thin. We try to help each other out whenever we can. Maybe I see an outfitter doing something illegal and can let Don know. And as you see, Don helps me catch poachers when he's available.

"But to answer your question, Will, each investigation is different. First, we go where the dead animal was found and try to get enough physical evidence to tie the animal's death to a particular person or persons. If we're lucky, the poacher will have left a bullet, parts taken from the animal, maybe a broken piece of knife. Whatever. If there's a piece of meat or a hide in someone's possession, we can take it and try to match it with some other part taken at the scene. We look to see if they have the same DNA."

"Wow," I said. "Just like on TV."

"TV makes things look easy," Carlos said. "But usually they're not. And these tests are spendy. If the case goes to court and the DNA of the animal part found at the scene is the same as the animal found in the accused person's possession, that person has to pay for the tests as part of their fine. It can add up to a lot of money."

Pete leaned his arms on the table and folded his big hands. "I once went with Carlos to investigate an illegally killed elk. It was amazing to watch him work. We looked for footprints, horse tracks, and how they took the elk meat. Carlos checked to see if it was cut with a knife, a hatchet, or a saw. All those things provided evidence."

"What do you do when you talk to people you think might be poachers?" Mom asked. "Is that pretty touchy?"

Carlos rubbed his hand over his Montana Department of Fish, Wildlife, and Parks patch with the brown grizzly bear. "Sometimes. I go into camps to see what people know. Some people are nervous around law enforcement officers anyway, so I have to try to make a good judgment call. If someone looks suspicious—not just nervous—I look into things more."

"Like what?" Jed asked.

"Like are there things around the camp associated with an illegally killed animal? Or say I go into a fishing camp and there's a rifle with a scope lying against a tree. That might be suspicious. But many people take rifles with them on trips, so having one in camp doesn't mean they're poachers or intend to do something illegal."

Oriole put her head on my boots. I reached down and patted her on the head. "So how do you find out if someone's telling the truth?"

"Sometimes it takes a while to get to the truth. One lie covers up another and they get in deeper. Often they can't remember what the last lie was.

"Once at Schafer Meadows, some guys at the horse camp got an elk. When I asked to see it, the guy who shot it wasn't too eager to talk to me. I asked to see the tag, which is required by law to be put on the animal after it's shot. He couldn't find the tag. Said it must have fallen off somewhere between where he killed the elk and the camp. We went to the kill site and looked. It wasn't there. Back at the camp I asked for his license. He was slow to open his wallet. The license wasn't there. 'Could it be in your tent?' I asked. 'Must be,' he said. It wasn't there, either. Finally, I said, 'Look. I know you don't have a license.' The guy had no more lies in him and finally said he'd illegally killed the elk."

Mom sat with one foot on her chair seat and her arm resting on her knee. "Seems like you have to be pretty patient with people in order to find the truth."

Dad grinned. "I've watched game wardens work with people, and sometimes patience isn't the only way they get to the truth. Sometimes things happen unexpectedly. Once in New Mexico I happened to be along while our law enforcement officer helped a game warden. They had set up a decoy—a fake deer—along a road and waited in some nearby bushes to see if someone would try to kill what they thought was a real deer. A big truck pulling a horse trailer came along. When the truck reached the decoy, a rifle appeared in the window and *blam!* The decoy was shot. The game warden jumped out of the bushes and got all the people out of the truck.

"There were four of them, a husband, wife, and two little kids. Our law enforcement officer knew the kids were frightened, so she stayed with them to try to keep them calm. One little girl watched as the warden handcuffed her father. She started to cry. 'Why are they taking my daddy away?' The law enforcement officer said, 'Because your daddy did something wrong and he has to go to jail for a few days.' The little girl said, 'But Daddy didn't shoot the deer. Mommy did.'"

Everyone cracked up at that.

Will stopped laughing long enough to ask what Carlos and Don had discovered about the dead deer and bear.

"I told you some of the ways we investigate, and after all that, there's still not much to report," Don said. "Except for the carcasses, both trails were pretty cold. Casey didn't smell out anything more with the deer than what he and Oriole had already discovered. And we found nothing else where the bear was killed. Whoever did this didn't leave clues. It's pretty frustrating."

"Do you think it's one person or more?" Mom asked.

"Hard to tell at the moment," Carlos said. "We can't be certain someone actually took the deer meat, although that seemed to be what they were after. Animals had pretty well picked the bones clean, and there wasn't any meat lying around. If all of it had been taken, I'd bet on more than one person. It would be a lot for someone to carry alone, although I'm sure it's been done."

Charlie whittled on the piece of wood he said was a surprise for me. It looked like some kind of animal. "It must make it more difficult for you to figure out how many people killed the bear because the only things taken were its paws," Charlie said. "If the hide and meat had been taken, too, you'd pretty well know more than one person did it. That was a good-sized bear and would have made a huge and heavy load."

"True," Carlos said, "unless they had good pack animals that could carry the meat and hide. Then a person could do it alone."

"Don't some horses and mules shy at carrying wild meat or dead things?" Jim asked. "I thought I'd heard that before."

"You'd better believe it," Pete said. "Once we watched some hunters try to load an elk they'd shot onto a 'green' pack mule—one not used to carrying strange or different things on its back. There was no way. It must not have liked the smell of wild meat or blood. That mule bucked and kicked and snorted and danced in circles every time they tried to lay a pack on its back. They finally put the elk on another mule that didn't seem to mind what kind of cargo it carried. The green mule settled down and allowed the hunters to load it with much heavier items, like food and gear. Go figure."

Carlos leaned down and patted Casey on the head. "This is a great dog for sniffing out bad guys," he said, "one a game warden like me would love to have. But even he needs help when there's not much to go on. Don and I plan to take Casey with us to check out a few more areas."

Great, I thought. *Allie and Will may be able to stay a bit longer.*

"You know," Jim said, "I promised these kids a plane ride. Why don't I take them up and look around at the same time? Maybe we can see who's traveling on trails in the area. We won't be able to pick out everyone, but it might help some."

"Yeah!" Will said. "Can we go, Dad? We can help. I know we can."

Don smiled and laid his hand on Will's shoulder. "We'll have to check with Allie's parents to make sure it's okay for her to fly, but it's okay with me. Jim's a great pilot."

Jim slapped his blue baseball cap with the airplane on it onto the table. "It's set then. If Allie can go, we'll leave tomorrow morning about ten or so. Most hikers or horse riders should be out and about by then."

"Oh, Jim, thanks. This is great!" I said, hugging him.

"Glad we can finally do it. And you might practice tonight with Oriole to make sure she'll keep that headset on."

Oriole heard her name and got up. Looking like she owned the world, she made a slow stately walk to Jim, put her head in his lap, and let him rub her ears.

"You mean she can go, too?" I asked.

"Of course. She's my co-pilot."

"Remind me not to fly with you," Charlie said, whittling away on his piece of wood. "Your choice of co-pilots leaves a lot to be desired."

"Well, Oriole's got the right stuff. Way more than you do, old man."

"I'll remember that the next time you ask me to navigate."

The Flight

"Jump in, Oriole," I said as Jim opened the plane door the next morning.

Oriole jumped in and settled herself down on the backseat.

"Sorry, but you've got to ride in the 'Wayback,' Oriole," Jim said. He patted the area behind the back seat. Oriole looked at him like he was crazy.

"C'mon, girl," I said, also patting behind the seat. "You've got a nice cushy foam pad in the back all to yourself—best seat in the house. You can still be Jim's co-pilot from there."

Oriole put her front paws on the back of the seat and pushed with her back legs. She hoisted herself up and slipped and slithered over the seat and into the rear of the plane. She looked as if she decided the foam pad would do.

I scratched her on the head. "Good dog, Oriole. Now show Jim how well you wear your new headset."

I placed the set on Oriole's head. She started to paw at her black ear and shake her head, but then stopped. She flopped down and curled up in a ball, leaving the headset in place.

Jim handed me a helmet with a built-in microphone and motioned for me to get into the back seat. "All right, Jessie. Looks like Oriole's ready to go. Let's get you three in now."

Jim had two other helmets in his arms. He held one up. "Okay, who's riding in back with Jessie?"

Will grabbed the helmet and pulled himself into the backseat. "I will. Allie's never gotten to fly over the wilderness before. She should have the best seat."

Allie grabbed the last helmet. "Hey, thanks, Will. Guess this means I have to be nice to you for a while. I'm sure glad my parents said I could fly. This is cool!"

I'd forgotten how loud a small plane can be when you're sitting inside listening to the engine rev up. And I'd forgotten how bumpy Shafer's grassy airstrip is. It feels kind of like a wild carnival ride where everyone is screaming. I looked back at Oriole, who lay on the foam pad with her head up, looking at me. The first time we flew with Jim, when we'd first come to Schafer Meadows, she'd stared at me with huge eyes when the plane took off, looking scared to death. This time she looked relaxed and didn't try to stand or put her head on the back of my seat. I reached for her, and she licked my hand.

Soon Jim had the plane in the air. I'd been so concerned about Oriole that I hadn't even noticed the bumpy grassy runway or heard the roar of the engine. I gave Oriole one more pat and turned to the window to enjoy the scenery.

We flew toward Scott Lake, following the trail where we found the poached deer. No one was on the trail.

Scott Lake looked beautiful from the air, with its marshy edges and lush green fir and spruce trees surrounding it. A small opening in the forest caught my eye. It looked like someone had put up a tan lean-to not far from the lake. I bet it made a great camp—private—because it was hidden in the forest, and yet close to the trail and lake.

Soon we flew over Flotilla Lake. A group of four men fished along the shore. The sun shimmered on the lake as a slight breeze skimmed across the water.

Jim bent his head to the left and looked down. "Beautiful day for fishing. Maybe we should have saved flying for another day."

Allie keyed her microphone. "Not if you ask me. I love to fish more than almost anything, but right now, flying in this plane with my friends is the only place I want to be."

Jim glanced into the back seat. "What about you two? Still want to fly?"

"You bet," Will said.

I reached back and patted Oriole on the shoulder. "We're all having fun."

Oriole sat up and got as close as she could to my side of the plane. She rested her head on the back of my seat and looked out the window. "No matter what Charlie says, I think you've got a good co-pilot, Jim. Oriole's loving this."

"Well, if everybody's having fun, let's keep going."

Jim banked the plane. We flew over Flotilla Lake with one wing pointing straight up and one straight down. It felt weird to fly sideways— like another crazy carnival ride—especially because the plane continued to turn. Allie braced herself at first but then got into it and gave Jim a huge smile. We got a good glimpse of the four fishermen as we passed over them, probably 500 feet above them. They waved at us, and when Jim righted the plane, the plane rocked back and forth.

Will gripped his seat. "Whoa! What was that?"

"Oh," Jim said. "Sorry if I scared you. There's nothing wrong with the plane. Pilots say hello to people below by rocking their wings. Maybe it seems a little odd, but no one can hear you when you're in the air, even if you shout."

Will let go of the seat. "Oh. Sure. Just so we're not having major turbulence. I'd hate to have to ask for a barf bag."

We flew back toward Schafer Meadows and veered off again.

"Where to now?" Allie asked.

"I thought we'd do a fly-by over the spot where the mother bear was found."

We flew up Schafer Creek and soon reached the trail junction where Oriole had rolled in some stinky part of the dead bear.

"See anything down there?" Jim asked.

Will was on the side of the plane nearest the junction. "Nope. Looks pretty quiet to me."

Jim circled the plane a couple of times so Allie and I could also take a look.

"I don't see anything," Allie said.

Oriole had found the bear not far off the trail and the trees formed a dense cover there, making it impossible to see underneath.

I looked as close as possible. "I don't see anything either."

It made me sad to think about the mother bear. She lost her life in this remote spot. We had a hard time even seeing where she died. As we circled, I wondered what happened to her cub. I imagined it wandering through the wilderness trying to fend for itself, scared and hungry. And too young to survive on its own. Tears started to well up in my eyes. Allie looked down and I saw tears in her eyes, too.

"Why did someone do this?" I asked. "How can they care so little for an animal that they would take its life without thinking of the consequences?"

Jim looked back at me. "Some people care only for themselves. They don't stop to think how their actions hurt others. This isn't an isolated instance of poaching. It happens all the time and all over the world. Birds are killed for their colorful feathers. Salmon for the price of their meat or eggs. Baby seals for their white fur. Alligators for their hides, and on and on. It's big bucks, and some people are selfish and greedy."

"Yeah," I said. "Last year I watched a TV show that said animals in Africa are losing ground to poachers. They're killing lots of animals with wire snares, poison arrows, spears, dogs, and firearms."

"What animals are they killing?" Allie asked.

"Oh, it varies by the area, but black rhinos are becoming extinct because poachers kill them for their horns. They don't even take the meat. And zebras and wildebeests are being hammered by poachers—tens of thousands each year. Their meat is sold to markets illegally. It's such good money that bush meat is even sold in neighboring countries."

"I hope they figure out how to stop the poaching there," Allie said. "Those animals are so beautiful. It would be horrible if they got wiped out by poachers."

Jim leveled the plane once again. "Let's go on toward Gooseberry. Maybe you'll feel better when you see the cabin from the air."

I sniffled and dried my eyes as Jim turned the plane up the Middle Fork River.

"Hey," Will said a few minutes later. "There's Gooseberry Cabin. It looks neat! And there's the barn and corral. They look lopsided from up here. Tiny, too."

Allie laughed. "And look up on the hill behind the cabin. There's the 'Out.' It really looks tiny. It's a good thing nobody had to go there right now. They'd be in for a surprise!"

I laughed, too, feeling better. "Yeah. Guess whoever built the 'Out' without walls or a ceiling never thought about planes flying overhead."

It was Jim's turn to laugh. "I bet a pilot or two has done a double-take when flying over this spot when they caught someone in the act. Well, let's fly up the Clack Creek Trail and see if anyone's up there."

We didn't get too far up the trail before Will pointed down. "Hey! It's those four backpackers. Looks like they're just leaving their camp."

Jim circled a large meadow with pockets of trees next to a creek. A couple of tents huddled under a small group of trees. Even though their camp looked tiny from the air, we could make out bags hanging from ropes tied high in the air between trees. The backpackers had stuffed their food into the bags, making sure no bears could steal it.

We followed the Clack Creek Trail, watching the back-packers march onward in single file. A large rocky mountain shaped like a giant triangle appeared in front of us.

"Pentagon Mountain," Jim said. "Look at the size of that monster. You can see it from lots of places in the wilderness, even from the ground."

We flew past Pentagon Mountain and saw a small lake below. "What's that called?" Allie asked.

"Dean Lake. Look at the blue-green color. Glaciers prob-ably carved it thousands of years ago and snow, rain, and ice continually fill it."

Oriole suddenly stood and wagged her tail. She looked in the direction of the lake. "Whatcha see, girl?" I asked.

Smoke from a small campfire rose in the air. Two people walked from the lake toward a small tan and yellow tent. A large dog followed behind. Oriole must have zeroed in on the dog, even though we flew high enough that the dog looked like a puppy.

"Hey!" I said. "That must be the people Lost ran into who had the dog with the bloody paws. Remember? He said he saw them near here."

Allie turned and grabbed the back of her seat to look at me. "Yeah. I bet you're right. That proves Lost saw those people and was telling the truth. I knew he was too good to be a poacher."

"Well," Jim said, "it doesn't prove that he's not a poacher, but it looks a lot better for him. How 'bout we head back to Schafer Meadows and report to Warden Carlos and Don, Will's dad?"

"And don't forget Casey," Will said. "He's the law dog. We should report to him, too."

Jim turned the plane back toward Clack Creek. The four backpackers had worked their way up the trail a bit farther. We flew toward the meadow where they had their camp. Close

to the camp I spotted another small opening in the trees near
Clack Creek. I thought I saw another tan lean-to, but it might
have been just a gravel bar surrounded by trees near the creek.
It looked out of place, though—gravel bars aren't smooth—so
I filed it away in my memory and looked out the window to
enjoy the flight.

Casey greeted us when we arrived, waggling around the
plane until Will climbed out and gave him a hug. Seeing Casey
meant that Don and Carlos had either not left to look for poachers or had already returned. Maybe we'd have a chance to talk
to them.

Oriole and Casey seemed content to trot to the cookhouse
rather than chasing each other all over the airstrip. Maybe
they were finally getting used to having each other around and
didn't feel like they had to go nuts every time they got together.
I felt content, too. Maybe I didn't need to worry anymore that
Will and Allie would have to go home. It was time to just enjoy
their friendship.

The cookhouse door slammed and Don and Carlos came
out just as we got there. Don hugged Will and reached down to
scratch Casey's muzzle. "Hey, son. How'd your flight go?" he
asked.

"Great," Will said.

"It was really cool," Allie said. "I can't believe how beautiful the mountains are from the air."

"See many people?"

"Not many. Only four fishermen at Scott Lake and those
four backpackers that stopped here for trail information."

"We also saw two people and a dog up by Dean Lake,"
Jim said.

"Oh yeah," Allie said. "I bet they were the people Lost
talked about seeing—the ones with the injured dog. That's
good, right? It means Lost isn't the poacher?"

Carlos shrugged. "Let's hope so. Uh, Jim, I've got a favor to ask. My boss wants to have a meeting in Kalispell tomorrow. He'd like Don to be there, too. Any chance you can fly us there? Fish and Game is willing to foot the bill."

"How soon do you need to go?"

"Tomorrow will be soon enough. The meeting's not scheduled 'til afternoon."

"No problem. I can check on a few things in town, fuel up while you're at your meeting, and bring you back whenever you're ready."

Carlos nodded to Don. "That work for you?"

Don ruffled Will's hair. "How 'bout it, buddy? Think you and Allie can stand staying here at Schafer Meadows another day? That is, if the Scott family will have you and it's okay with Allie's folks."

I grinned. "I know Mom and Dad won't care. They're glad to have Will and Allie around to keep me out of trouble."

"Well, let's go ask them," Don said.

"Yahoo!" Allie said. She did a little dance.

The next morning, we watched Jim and his plane take off with Carlos and Don. Will waved with both arms as Jim circled and rocked his wings. Oriole and Casey barked and chased each other.

"Well, now what?" Allie asked.

"Now what?" Will said. "You can't sit still for one minute?"

"You can if you want to, but I plan to make the most of my time here. What do you say we go swimming in the river, Jessie?"

"Sure. You coming, Will, or is this too much for you in one day?"

"Of course I'm coming. I wouldn't want to miss hearing you two scream when you hit that freezing water."

Twenty minutes later, bathing suits under our clothes, we grabbed our towels and hopped off the porch. Oriole and Casey barked excitedly as if they knew they were going swimming, too. I stuck my head in the cookhouse door where Mom and Charlie sat at the kitchen table. Dad and Pete had gone to talk with an outfitter whose horses had escaped from his camp. I told Mom we'd see them later.

I no sooner closed the door than tall Ben Morris and his horse and mule rode up. This time Oriole didn't go near his horse, maybe remembering it had tried to bite her earlier. Instead she made a beeline for the side of the cookhouse, with Casey in tow.

"Hi, Mr. Morris," I said. "Back already?"

"Yep. Summer's too short and it's too pretty in the wilderness to spend much time anywhere else."

I noticed his mule had a light pack load again.

"Planning to stay long?"

Ben hesitated, and his piercing eyes locked onto mine. "Long as I need to."

"Well, have a good trip. Be seeing ya."

Ben nodded and turned his horse toward the trail. The sun flashed on something on his neck as he rode by. My breath caught in my throat. I stifled a gasp.

Around his neck, Ben wore a necklace with a single bear claw on it.

FIFTEEN

On the Trail

I motioned to Will and Allie to follow me and hurried around the corner of the cookhouse. I nearly tripped over Oriole and Casey, who lay sprawled in the shade of the building. Putting my finger to my lips, I tiptoed to the side of the cookhouse, peeked around the corner to make sure Ben had kept on moving, and turned back to Will and Allie.

"Did you see that?" My voice was an octave higher than normal as I tried to whisper.

"How could we miss it?" Allie said, shaking and stamping her feet like someone just told her she'd won a million dollars. "That claw was huge!"

"Yeah. What was he thinking, wearing that thing?" Will asked, apparently trying to keep his voice down but finding it hard, too. "He might as well have worn a huge sign that said *Poacher.*"

We looked around the corner of the cookhouse. If Ben had turned in his saddle, he'd have seen three heads staring at him, lined up one above the other like heads on a totem pole. Thankfully he didn't.

We ducked back once more.

"I think it's safe to talk," I said. "Ben must be out of earshot by now."

"What do we do?" Allie asked.

"I don't know what we can do until my dad and Carlos come back from their meeting," Will said. "Man, I wish we'd asked Ben where he was going."

"Did you see how light his mule's packs were?" I said.

Will nodded. "I bet you he's our poacher. That claw probably came from the mother bear."

"I bet you're right," Allie said, bouncing up and down. "But we can't be a hundred percent sure. We need proof."

I had an idea. "Maybe we can get proof. Maybe Ben's headed to the horse camp. I've snooped around there enough to know we can hide out and see someone without them knowing we're there. Better yet, if he's there, we can go swimming and watch him at the same time."

"Great idea," Will said. "Let's go."

"Don't you think you should tell your parents what we're doing first, Jessie?" Allie asked.

"Huh-uh. Not yet. My dad and Pete are gone, and Mom's hard at work on her book. My dad and Pete are gone, and Mom's busy talking to Charlie about her book."

Allie waved her hands in front of each other. "Wait a minute. Wait a minute. I don't know about catching any poacher. Remember how dangerous your dad said poachers can be? I don't think we should mess with one."

"I don't either," I said. "And I don't mean we should actually catch him. We can see what he's up to at the horse camp and then tell my dad or Don and Warden Carlos later. I've got really strong binoculars. We can take turns watching him from a distance."

Will snapped his towel at us. "C'mon. We're wasting time."

We sprinted up the Big River Trail and raced down the narrow side trail that enters into a large grassy meadow along the river. People with horses and mules often stay there because it has enough room for them and their animals and the river provides good water. The horse camp was deserted. Ben was nowhere in sight.

Allie flopped to the ground, panting. "Great! Now what?"

I dropped next to her. Oriole and Casey stuck their noses in my face, nearly knocking me over. I put my arms out in front of me to ward them off. "Cut it out, you two. Can't you see I'm dying here?"

The dogs flattened me, tails wagging as they tried to lick me. I couldn't help laughing as I squirmed to get away from them. I finally caught my breath. "Well, we can always go swimming. We promised Oriole and Casey a fun afternoon."

Will kicked at a rock stuck in the ground. "I've got a better idea. Let's go back to the Big River Trail and try to pick up Ben's tracks. At least they'd tell us which direction he headed. If he went up the trail, we can come back here for our swim, because he'd be too far ahead to catch up to him. But if he crossed the Middle Fork, we can follow his tracks and see if he went up Schafer Creek or turned up the Dolly Varden Trail near where Oriole found the dead mother bear. And when your dad and Pete get back, Jessie, we can tell them which way he went."

We ran up the trail from the horse camp to the Big River Trail.

Allie got there first. "No sign of any recent tracks. Let's keep looking."

Off we ran again, back toward Schafer Meadows. I thought my lungs would burst. At the trail junction to the river, Will bent over and put his hands on his knees, breathing hard. "It's a good thing…we got here…when we did…I don't think I…could have…run…anymore."

We took a good look at the ground by the trail junction. A clear set of fresh tracks turned toward the river. Large prints from a shod horse and mule gave us a pretty good clue that Ben had gone that way.

"Hurry up," I said. "Maybe we can catch up to him."

"No way, Jessie," Allie said. "He had a huge head start. Unless he stopped to enjoy the scenery, he's long gone."

"Yeah, you're probably right. But like Will said, we should follow Ben's tracks and at least see which way he went on the other side. I mean I think we need to see if he passed by where Oriole found the dead bear."

Oriole streaked past us. She stopped and turned to face us, planting all four legs. Her chest heaved and her eyes sparkled with delight and mischief as she looked beyond us. Casey caught up to her and bowled her over. Both dogs went tumbling down a hill off the trail. When they returned to the trail, Oriole's normally shiny yellow coat and all her black parts were a dirty dull tan. Casey's black Lab fur had turned dusty brown. Both looked like mangy strays. They panted hard for a moment and then raced off again.

We reached the river's edge, quickly put on our sandals that we'd carried in a daypack with our towels, and plunged into water to our knees. I turned to say something to Allie but the icy water took my breath away. With what strength I had left, I sloshed through the freezing current, carefully picking my way across the slick round river rocks. I didn't want to fall down.

My legs had turned red and felt numb by the time we got to the other side. I sat at the river's edge and rubbed them to warm them up before putting my hiking socks and boots back on. Will and Allie did the same.

"I don't think I want to swim here when we come back," Allie said. "That river feels colder than it did when we had our water fight. Must be the weather. We'd better get moving."

"Yeah," Will said, "but there's no sense in killing ourselves trying to catch up to Ben. He's got at least an hour start on us."

We slowed the pace to a near crawl, regaining our breath. When we reached the trail junction where Oriole had found the dead mother bear, the horse tracks turned up the Dolly Varden Trail. Oriole went into the woods where she found the dead bear, taking Casey with her. We followed the dogs. Both of them sniffed the area all over, although now there was no visible sign of the bear, not even a strand of fur.

Oriole started to bend her knees like she was going to lie down.

"Don't you dare roll again!" I shouted, remembering how she had rolled on the dead bear carcass. I had to bathe her three times in dog shampoo to get rid of the smell of rotten meat.

Oriole looked guilty, stood up, and then sat by my side.

"Good girl. I know your instincts tell you to cover up your own smell with another animal's. But—yecch—you just can't put 'Essence of Dead Bear' perfume behind your ears and along your neck and back. It's too stinky."

I let out a big sigh. "Guess we might as well go back to Schafer and wait for the 'Arm of the Law' to arrive. Too bad we didn't find Ben or catch him in the act."

"Yeah," Allie said, "but at least we've got some good stuff to tell Tom—uh, your dad, Jessie—and Pete when they get back."

When we got back to Schafer in mid-afternoon, Dad and Pete still hadn't returned from helping the outfitter whose horses had escaped. I felt like I had a huge secret and no one to tell it to. Charlie was off somewhere. Mom left a note saying she'd gone for a walk. And Don and Carlos were in Kalispell at their meeting. All we could do was sit and wait for someone— anyone—to get back.

Meanwhile, we sat in my living room and talked about Ben and our suspicions that he was the poacher.

"Look," Will said, stretching out his legs and bare feet on the couch. "Ben was in the area where the deer was poached and also where the mother bear was killed."

Allie sat cross-legged on the floor, leaning against the couch. Oriole lay on her back with her legs in the air on one side of Allie, and Casey lay on his back on her other side. Allie absentmindedly rubbed both dogs' bellies while the dogs groaned in ecstasy. "And," she said, leaning forward, "don't forget that every time we've seen Ben he's arrived with light manty packs and left with heavy ones."

I curled up my bare feet on an easy chair, stretched my arms above my head, and yawned. "Yeah. That seems the strangest thing of all. What possible reason could Ben have for having fuller packs when he leaves than when he gets here? He's not working for an outfitter who takes dudes on wilderness trips and carries their stuff out."

"And he's not fishing," Allie said.

"Even if he were fishing, he couldn't possibly catch that many fish—not legally anyway—and it would sure stink when he carried them out."

Will curled into a ball on the couch and plumped a couch pillow under his head. He stifled a yawn. "Well, we're not getting anywhere. I think I'll close my eyes and think on it."

The screen door squeaked open and closed with a bang. I had dozed off in the chair and bolted upright. Will jerked awake from the couch. Allie lay sprawled out on the floor like the middle of a dog sandwich. Oriole lay on her side with her back to Allie, and Casey had his head on Allie's stomach. Oriole lazily lifted her head to see what the noise was all about before flopping back down with a groan. Normally, the dogs would be electrified at the first sound of the door opening. Guess we wore them out.

"Well. I see you three are making the most of your time together." Dad put his saddlebags on the floor by the door and grinned at us.

"We've been waiting for you to get home," I said. "We've got lots to tell you."

Dad sat next to Will on the couch. "So what's been happening while I was away?"

"We think we know who the poacher is."

Allie sat up and leaned back on her arms. "Yeah. We've got some pretty good evidence."

Dad scrunched up his face and tilted his head. "What have you kids been up to?"

I jumped off my chair and sat next to Allie on the floor. Oriole put her paw on my leg. "Nothing, Dad, honest. We've just seen things that are hard to explain and put two and two together."

"Okay, so tell me what you've seen."

We told Dad about Ben and how each time he came into the wilderness he had light packs on his mule but left with full ones.

"Yeah," Will said, "and don't you think it's weird that he comes and goes so much? It takes a long time to get anywhere in the wilderness if you go in far enough. Why would he leave just to turn around and come right back in again?"

Allie stood up. "And Ben just came back this afternoon after having left a few days ago. His manties were light again, and guess what he had around his neck?"

Together Allie and I blurted out, "A bear claw necklace!"

"Oh, Dad," I said. "You should've seen it. He wears it on a leather thong and it's got just one claw. It's kinda cool and gross at the same time."

Allie nodded. "And he rode up the trail where Oriole found the mother bear."

"How do you know that?" Dad asked. "You kids weren't following him, were you?"

I looked at the floor. "Well, maybe a little."

Dad frowned and I knew a lecture was coming. I figured I'd better speak first.

"We knew you wouldn't be happy with us getting in the way, so we just watched to see what he was doing. Anyway, he was way ahead of us, so after seeing his tracks turn up the trail we came back here to tell someone."

Dad sat quietly for a moment. "You three need to make sure you're not getting involved in this poaching thing. That's for Don and Carlos to worry about. It's dangerous. You may be kids, but poachers won't care. You could get hurt—or killed. I want to make it clear that you should stay away."

He stood up. "You've got some good points about Ben, but they don't prove he's the poacher. There might be very good reasons why he's traveling lightly coming into the wilderness and leaving with a heavy load. And it's not illegal for someone to wear a bear claw necklace. When Don and Carlos get here you can tell them your story. Maybe they have a way of finding out what Ben's been up to on his trips back here. Meanwhile, I want you kids to stay well away from Ben Morris. Stop snooping around."

"Don't worry, Dad," I said. "We didn't want to get involved—it just happened. All we want to do is have fun."

Dad opened the screen door and stood to the side. "Then why don't you go out and do it?"

SIXTEEN

The Load

A loud *crack* of the bat meant Jed had hit a homer. We had found Jed cleaning out the tool shed and talked him into spending the rest of the afternoon playing a poor game of four-person baseball on the airstrip. It wasn't really baseball because all we had was a pitcher, a batter, and two fielders. But we had fun trying to catch ground balls that headed straight for us and then hit some dirt clod and bounced away. Oriole and Casey stole the ball over and over and played keep-away with us. We made a rule that whoever tagged the dog with the ball automatically scored a run, whether they were the batter or not. The dogs got the ball so often that we decided even the batter could tag the dog instead of running the bases to score. We had people running all over the airstrip trying to catch the dogs. Not exactly Major League rules, but we didn't care.

After dinner we heard the drone of a plane engine get louder and louder. Soon a small white plane with a blue top circled the airstrip. The pilot knew to look for people or animals on the strip before landing. A mother moose and her baby, munching grass, did a stiff-legged trot into the shelter of the forest next to the runway before the plane landed. Jim, Don, and Warden Carlos got out, grabbed their gear from the back compartment, and dropped it on the picnic table outside the cookhouse.

"My boss made this poaching business my top priority," Carlos said. He swung his leg over the bench of the table and sat down. "He's afraid other animals may get killed if we don't find the poacher soon."

Dad sat next to Carlos, his elbows resting on the table top. "These kids have some information that may help you."

Way to go Dad, I thought. *You took us seriously.* Will and Allie gave each other a silent "high five."

Once again we told what we knew—that Ben Morris always came into the wilderness with light packs and left with full ones, that he came and went often, and that he wore a bear claw necklace the last time he came in.

Carlos slapped away a fly that landed on his pant leg. "Don't get your hopes up. There could be lots of reasons for his actions. But maybe it's time to pay Ben a visit—if we can find him."

"Oh, I bet you'll find him," I said. "He doesn't stay in the wilderness for very long. And we've got a good idea where he was headed. I bet he's back here no later than tomorrow."

"Right," Will said. "That seems to be about as long as he stays."

Carlos drummed his fingers on the table. "We'll head out tomorrow morning and see if we can round him up in case he doesn't come back. Meanwhile, if you kids spot him before we do, stay away from him. Tom, will you be here tomorrow?"

Dad nodded. "Yep. I'll be around all day."

"Tom's the ranger here. You kids let him know where Ben is if he shows up before we do and we'll take it from there. We won't lose him—I promise."

I awoke the next morning thinking someone was trying to shake me awake. Oriole lay sprawled at the bottom of my bed. Her legs twitched against mine in some dream as she whimpered first softly and then louder. Not wanting to wake her, I lazed in bed, listening to a light pattering rain on the roof. Distant thunder rumbled. I hoped we didn't get a lot of rain. Will, Allie, and I had plans to visit a family from Idaho who were on an extended backpacking trip. The parents had stopped at the cookhouse after we had dinner last night and talked with Jim and Charlie. They have a boy and girl about our age we wanted to meet. The family planned to stay in the campground until after breakfast and then would be on their way. If it rained hard enough, they'd either hurry and go or stay longer to wait out the storm. No way of knowing what they'd decide to do.

The rain continued to fall, getting louder. It alternated between spurts of heavy drops and light drizzle. Oriole woke up, arched her back in a huge stretch, yawned loudly, and thumped her tail a couple of times. She didn't seem too eager to get out of bed.

I scratched her lightly on her chest. "What's the matter, girl? Weather got ya down?"

Her eyelids drooped, and her tail thumped weakly a couple more times. She pulled her paws to her nose in a tight bunch and stretched again. Then she stood up suddenly and shook, starting at her head and ending with the tip of her tail.

I laughed. "You must be ready for your breakfast. Let's get up and find your buddy Casey, see if he's out and about yet."

Oriole bounded off the bed. Her toenails clattered on the wooden floor as she danced in small circles, trying to get me to move faster. I threw on a pair of old jeans and a long-sleeved tan T-shirt with cartoon dogs in running shoes on the front. I followed Oriole out of the bedroom. She scrambled down the stairs and jumped on the couch, which had been made into a bed. Allie shrieked from under the covers while Oriole stood over her and tried to nose her out of bed.

Allie threw the covers over her head. "Not funny, Oriole. I was in the middle of a great dream about not having to go to school this fall because my grades were so good."

Oriole nudged her again.

"Sorry," I said. "Looks like the dog alarm clock has gone off and doesn't have a snooze button. Might as well get up. She's not going to let you stay in bed any longer."

Allie threw the covers off her head. Her hair stood out in all directions.

I laughed. "Ooohh! Talk about a bad hair day."

She touched her hair. I heard a loud snap.

Allie scowled. "Ouch! Static electricity and dog breath. Eeoooww! What a way to wake up. Where are my glasses?"

I found Allie's glasses on a little round wooden table next to the couch and handed them to her. She pulled herself out from under Oriole and slid into a sitting position. "Think that Idaho family will still be in the campground?"

"Hard telling. Let's go find Will and Casey and see if they want to go there with us. Better grab your raincoat and boots, though. It's really coming down."

We splashed across the lawn to the large canvas tent behind our house where Will and Don bunked with Warden Carlos. Rain poured off the tent, sending rivers of water down the sides. Drops of water that hit the ground splashed back upward. I hoped it was dry inside. Allie and I hollered, but no one answered back.

Next stop was the cookhouse. Outside, we took off our dripping raincoats, shook them, and hung them on wooden pegs beside the door before going inside.

The screen door banged shut behind us. Will, his dad Don, Warden Carlos, and my dad sat at the long kitchen table. Charlie came in from the office in the back.

Carlos glanced up from a map laid in front of him. "You kids are sure about the trail Ben took when he came in last time?"

I traced a red dashed line on the map with my finger. "That's the trail, all right. Here's where Oriole found the mother bear."

Allie agreed. "Yeah. We saw his tracks heading up the trail past there."

Dad pointed to a spot a little farther up the trail. "There's a camp not far from there where an outfitter brings clients to stay while they hunt in the fall. Do you suppose Ben might have headed there?"

"It's possible, but I'm not sure why," Carlos said. "If he's working for the outfitter, it doesn't make sense. It's nowhere near hunting season, so the outfitter wouldn't have a reason to use the camp. And if Ben went there now, he'd find it deserted—no tents, people—nothing."

Charlie leaned over the map. "If he's the poacher, maybe that's why he'd go there. He'd have the place to himself. It's not that far to go if you want to take a look. You could be back by lunchtime."

"Might as well go then," Carlos said. "Maybe we'll get lucky."

Will, Allie, and I decided to visit the Idaho family at the campground after Carlos and Don left to look for Ben. We trailed behind them to the barn with Dad and Pete. Casey and Oriole trotted along with us.

Don and Carlos had just finished feeding and watering their horses when a lone rider on a tall horse with a big mule appeared from out of the misty fog brought on by the rain. He rode the trail that goes behind the barn toward the cookhouse.

Ben Morris wore a full-length dark brown oilskin rain slicker. He had a clear plastic rain cover over a black cowboy hat. He came to a complete stop on the trail as Carlos slowly approached him. Ben nodded a hello and rain ran off his hat like water from a faucet.

"Hi," Carlos said. "How's it going?"

Ben shifted in his saddle. His penetrating dark eyes seemed to bore into Carlos. "Not bad if it don't rain."

Don came up and stood next to Ben's big mule. The sopping mule shook itself, sounding like someone shaking a huge piece of canvas. Water sprayed everywhere.

"Beautiful animal," Don said, wiping water from his face. "He must be able to carry quite a load."

Ben shifted his eyes to Don. "Been known to carry more'n a couple hunnerd pounds when I've asked him."

"Not bad. Looks like you've got a pretty good load on him now," Don said.

"It's lighter'n it looks."

All this time Oriole and Casey had circled the big mule, their noses in the air. Oriole kept a close watch on the big horse that had tried to bite her, but the mule ignored the two dogs walking and sniffing around it. Ben pulled on his horse's ropes as it started to prance. Its hooves squished loudly in the wet mud. The horse turned to face the dogs and put its head down and ears back, looking like it wanted another go at Oriole. Ben's rough-looking hands with broken dirty nails pulled tighter on the reins.

Carlos laid a hand on one of the manty tarp loads tied to the mule. "What are you carrying?"

"Oh, just a bunch o' junk I'm takin' out."

"Well, these two dogs sure seem interested in what you have in there. Mind if we have a look?"

Ben's eyes turned to slits as he looked from Carlos to Don to Dad and back again. "What, did I do something wrong?"

Carlos took out his badge. "Game warden. Seems someone's interested in taking some of our wildlife out of the wilderness—illegally. I'd like to take a look at your packs, check what's in the mule's load. If you don't mind, that is. You can tie up to the hitch rail and we'll get this over with fast. If everything's junk as you say, you can be on your way."

I put my hand to Will's ear and whispered. "What if Ben won't do it? Can Carlos make him?"

"No," Will whispered. "He'll have to get a search warrant. That could take days, especially with us here in the wilderness and the warrant being in Kalispell, miles away by trail. Now, ssshhhh! I want to hear this. This is cool!"

Ben pursed his lips but then shrugged and turned his horse and mule toward the hitch rail. "You want to see what I've got? Suit yourself."

He slid down from his horse and slapped the reins so hard on the hitch rail that they made a loud snapping noise and wound around the rail twice before coming to a stop. He tied the horse and the mule separately to the rail. He stood to one side, bowed, and swept one arm to the side, palm up.

"Be my guest," Ben said through clenched teeth.

Carlos grabbed the end of the big mule's rope from the hitch rail and gave it a yank. The knot came free. "Let's take the mule to the barn so we don't soak everything inside the manties."

We kids slogged through the mud behind them. We stood just outside the door to stay out of their way. The dark gray sky continued to drop its load of water. Huge drops splattered to the ground outside the barn, creating large puddles.

Inside the barn, Carlos and Don lifted a manty the size of a large luggage bag from the mule. They had to stand on tiptoe to untie the rope securing the pack to the mule's pack saddle because the mule was so tall. When the heavy load finally slid to the ground, Dad motioned to Pete to grab one end while he took the other. They carried it away from the mule and dropped it. Pete sneezed when the pack hit the dirt floor, sending up a cloud of dust.

Don and Carlos took the second pack off the mule and dropped it on the barn floor with a loud *thunk.*

"Whoa," I whispered to Will and Allie. "What do you think's inside to make a noise like that? Metal leg traps? Saws? Knives?"

"I don't know," Allie whispered back. "It's too hard to tell from here. Can we go see?"

A strong smell of hay filled the barn. We moved against an inside wall and scrambled up on some hay bales to get a better view of the action. Fog rolled in the door of the barn and through slits between the dark brown wall logs. I shuddered, not sure if it was from the cold or from anticipation of what they'd find in the manties.

The four men began to unwrap the wet canvas manties that had turned from white to gray from much use. Ben leaned against a wall with folded arms and crossed legs. If looks could kill we'd have all been dead.

Dad and Pete carefully took the canvas cover off their manty. An open rectangular wooden box lay at an angle to the four corners of the square canvas placed flat on the ground. Dad stooped and searched through the contents of the box while Carlos and Don did the same with their manty.

We kids got off the hay bales and edged closer to get a better look.

I felt the blood drain from my head when I stared into the boxes.

SEVENTEEN

Answers

"Junk," Pete said, bending over and picking up a rusted tomato can. "Just like you said. Broken camp chairs and parts of a backpack frame." He grabbed a short wooden stick and stuck it into the box, lifting out a torn flannel shirt. "And weeds and garbage—plastic bags with eggshells, foil, and a bacon wrapper. I bet it's the garbage that attracted the dogs."

Ben unfolded his arms and pushed himself away from the wall with one foot. He walked toward the opened packs.

"Told you. I'm not a thief. And I'm definitely not a poacher."

That was the longest speech I'd heard Ben say, and it definitely wasn't one I wanted to hear. He was supposed to say "I'm guilty! I did it!"

Dad stood, looking confused and upset. "Ben, we're really sorry. How 'bout coming with us to the cookhouse so we can talk about this?"

Ben let out an exasperated sigh. "What for? So you can tell me what a nice guy I am? Soothe your own bruised egos?"

"Please, Ben. We feel horrible about this. We don't usually accuse someone without thinking we have the facts right. But this time we really made a mistake. Please, let's talk."

I trailed behind everyone as we moved to the cookhouse. My stomach was queasy. How could I have been so wrong about Ben? Everything pointed to him as the poacher—the empty packs that became full later, Ben's bear claw necklace. He even showed up at the right places where poaching had just occurred.

I looked at Will and Allie, and although they didn't appear as upset as I was, they both hung their heads as they walked. The Idaho campers we planned to visit never entered my mind.

"Sit down, Ben." Carlos pointed to a chair at the table. "Please."

Pete held up the coffee pot. "Can I pour you a cup?"

Ben crossed one leg over the other and folded his hands across his lap. "No thanks, I, uh—well, okay. Why not?"

He seemed to relax a bit. It's amazing how a cup of coffee can break the tension for some adults. I never could figure that one out.

Ben sipped his coffee. "What do you want to know?"

Carlos sat next to Ben at the end of the table. "Mostly, how'd you come by that junk and other stuff you have in your manties?"

Dad folded his hands behind his head. "And why?"

Ben looked around the room at all of us. He seemed to take a particularly long time when his eyes passed over Allie, Will, and me, but I might have imagined it because I felt so guilty. He reached down and patted both Oriole and Casey, who leaned against his legs, probably hoping to get their ears scratched.

"Well," Ben said, "I been comin' to the Great Bear Wilderness purt near ever' year since the mid '70s. I started out wranglin' horses for an outfit outta East Glacier, savin' money to send home to my folks in Billings. Neither of 'em was well, and I wanted to help as much as possible.

"I was a young 'un with lots o' energy. I'd never been to the wilderness before, and it got in my blood from the moment I hit that first trail."

Ben's dark eyes softened. He looked off as if remembering something wonderful and he seemed to mellow by the second.

"Huh. Haven't talked this much in a long time. Must need to get this off my chest. Hope you got the time."

Carlos topped off Ben's coffee cup. "We got the time. Please—go ahead."

"Where was I? Oh, yeah. I worked hard wranglin' that first summer and saved every penny. I felt so proud and knew my folks'd be proud, too. Didn't matter much, though. Both my parents took a turn for the worse whilst I was away and when I got home to Billings at the end of the summer, they was already gone. They died days apart from each other. Musta been while I was ridin' out of the Great Bear with a pocket full o' dough."

He looked down at his coffee cup and heaved a huge sigh. "Something died in me then or maybe just turned hard. I don't know. I felt such anger, like the world had gone against me. The same outfit offered me a job next summer but it was hard to go back to work for them. Thought the death of my folks might bring back bad memories. So I took a job with another dude ranch. The people I worked for the first year were great, and I expected to feel the same about the next outfit. But those people weren't so upright and honest. Not that they cheated dudes who went on their trips or anything—they didn't do that—but they cut corners every way they could think of when tryin' to beat the feds."

"What do you mean, Ben?" Dad asked.

Ben smiled but his eyes looked sad as he faced Dad. "Must be hard for you being a federal employee and all, especially as a ranger in this incredible place, huh? You got a great job until someone breaks the rules or tries to get away with things, right?"

Dad frowned but nodded in agreement.

"Well, the ranger back then had his hands full. You see, the feds changed the rules around the mid '70s because of the creation of the Wilderness Act. Until then, an outfitter could take as many people, horses, and mules as he wanted. Some outfits had nigh on 60 head of animals at times—way too many. The Wilderness Act cut down the number of saddle horses and pack mules to 25 per party. They also outlawed using chainsaws in wilderness areas."

Warden Carlos nodded. "Oh, yeah. There were lots of angry people back then. Change sometimes comes hard."

Pete reached for the coffee pot. "Some people might not have liked it, but others were happy. They thought the Wilderness Act helped keep wilderness areas from overuse. But we're getting away from your story. What happened next?"

Ben eased down into his chair and crossed his feet over his long straight legs. "Well, the people I worked for made a practice of tryin' to take in more clients, horses, and mules than they was allowed. Kept the feds busy tryin' to catch 'em. And they absolutely hated having to break down their camps at the end of the season and haul out what they knew they'd have to haul back in the next year."

Ben stopped talking and scratched Oriole and Casey's ears. His eyes seemed far away as if remembering that time. Finally he raised his head and continued. "Part of my job was to cache things my bosses didn't want to have to pack out."

We kids sat at the other end of the table, listening. I grabbed a napkin and wrote: "*Cache = stash, not $$.*"

Allie formed a big "O" with her mouth as Ben went on. "I don't know if they could see the anger and hurt in me or what, but I was the only one they asked to cache anything. I knew the Wilderness Act made caching illegal, but I didn't care. My anger got in the way.

"I got to be pretty good at it. Hiding camp furniture, bed frames, and cans of food behind trees or under brush far from trails was no problem for me. I got so good at it that even the folks I worked for couldn't find the caches. Only once did I nearly get caught. I was just finishing up buryin' a 50-gallon drum filled with grain and pellets for the horses and mules and coverin' it with a huge log when the ranger rode around the corner. I liked to died. Musta jumped a mile. He stopped and asked me what I was doin'. I told him I found this great piece of firewood and had dragged it out to saw it up. Didn't have my saw with me, but he didn't seem to notice. So I got away with it."

Ben smiled at the memory. "Anyway, I worked for that outfit another couple years before finally getting a fulltime job on a ranch east of the Continental Divide. After that I took my vacations in the wilderness. Couldn't stay away. I also couldn't keep from lookin' for things I'd cached. See, that outfit went out of business and never recovered some of their buried belongings. I didn't want to dig them up, just wanted to see if they were still there—kind of a game for me. And they were."

"Wow," Will said. "You mean your stuff's been there all this time? No one ever found any of it?"

"That's right," Ben said. "Like I said, I became an expert at how to hide things in the wilderness. Everything went along the same for years—until a couple years ago. I was ridin' along a bank on the Middle Fork River and came upon one of my hiding places. A piece of iron was stickin' out of the ground. The earth around a big ol' heavy iron camp stove I'd buried had given way. The rusty frame was half in the river.

"Something snapped in me. I love that river! I can't ride by without feelin' how lucky I am to see its crystal-clear waters, knowin' it's cleaner than most rivers, and hopin' it'll stay that way for a long time. That rusting stove was helpin' degrade the water."

Ben shook his head. "What I'd done made me sick," he said. "I decided right then to do somethin' about it to make amends for harming this beautiful land. Sam, my mule, can carry heavy and awkward loads, so I made up my mind to start haulin' out everything I could still find from those caches years ago."

Ben leaned forward in his seat. He held out his hands as if pleading with us to understand. "I love this wilderness and want to do right by it. My stuff from the past's purt near hauled out, but sometimes I run into weeds—mostly oxeye daisies. If they're anywhere close to a cache, they end up in manties with the rest of the junk."

He set his cup on the table and sat back. "Guess that's about it."

Don put his cup down, too. "So what do you think got the dogs all interested in your packs?"

"Oh. Hmm. All I can think is last night I had a steak for dinner. I like 'em purty rare. The bone went in a garbage bag that had daisies in it. The bag might not have been sealed tight enough."

Pete nodded. "Yep. One manty had a big plastic bag in it with daisies and a bone. The bag must have broken wide open. Plus, don't forget there was that bacon wrapper in there."

Ben patted Oriole and Casey again. "Your dogs sure have a strong sense of smell to sniff through a manty that high on a mule. Most aren't that good."

"They're great," Will said. "Dad uses Casey on law enforcement stuff because his nose is so good, and Casey's teaching Oriole."

"Yeah," I said. "It was partly their noses sniffing around you, and partly the bear claw necklace you have on, and partly the fact that you kept coming into the wilderness with light packs and leaving with full ones that made us kids think you were the poacher."

I looked down at my feet, unable to look into his eyes. "Can I ask you one question, Mr. Morris?"

Ben actually smiled. "Sure, so long as you keep it light."

"There was a mother bear killed not long ago, and when you came into the wilderness this time you had on that bear claw necklace. We thought you killed the bear and got the claw from it, but now I know we were wrong. Would it be okay to ask where you got it?"

Ben reached for the necklace with his thumb and stretched the leather thong so we could see it better. "Over the years I made friends with some people from the Blackfeet Nation in Browning, just north of here. One of 'em makes beautiful Native American jewelry. Lots of beaded bracelets and belts. He gave this necklace to me as a gift after I helped him nurse his favorite horse back to health when it was near death. It's a gift I cherish."

Once more I looked at my feet. "I'm really sorry."

"Me, too," Allie and Will said together.

"Well," Ben said, "it wasn't fun gettin' pulled over by the law as if I'd done somethin' wrong, but it feels pretty good right now to have finally told someone what I done all those years ago. I'm sorry for what I done to harm the wilderness. I plan to keep comin' back to make it better than it is now—to make it like it was before I got involved with that outfit. To do that, I gotta clean up my own mess."

Carlos stuck out his hand to Ben. "You're well on your way, I'd say. Thanks for being honest with us."

Dad shook Ben's hand, too. "Tell you what," he said. "If you have more caches around and can use some hands to clean them up, I'll be glad to get help for you."

"I'll help," I said. "And I bet Will and Allie will, too. There aren't many people like us who get to see the wilderness and understand how neat it is. I don't want to take it for granted."

"Yeah," Will said. "Maybe we'd find something valuable, like money or a treasure. Wouldn't that be cool?"

"Thanks, but believe it or not, this is my last load. And in all the junk I've hauled out, I never found anything worth sellin'. Just useless items that go to the dump. I'll be back to enjoy campin' in cache-free sites now and again, and I'll take out more weeds if I find 'em when I do." Ben grinned. "Unless pulling weeds is considered poaching."

We all laughed at that.

I still felt bad that we'd wronged Ben, but I thought maybe he could make me feel a little better. "Do you mind if I ask you another question?" I said.

"Go ahead."

"We kids were so sure you were the poacher, so we've kept our eyes open. Have you run into many other people while you've traveled around?"

"A few. Some outfitters comin' and goin'. A couple people campin' and fishin' the river. Four backpackers. And, oh yeah—one guy who travels alone with a huge backpack who seems not to have a clue where he is."

"Lost," I said.

"I suppose he is," Ben said.

We kids laughed.

"Oh, no," Allie said. "That's just what his friends call him."

"Oh. Well. Can't think of any others except for the trail crew." Ben smiled. "And you kids."

Don stood from the table. "And you kids seem to have gotten involved way over your heads. I want you to stay out of this."

We walked back to the barn. Dad, Pete, and Don helped Ben put the manties back on his mule. The men shook hands with Ben.

Don said, "We're sorry, Ben—all of us. We'll try to make sure these kids don't bother you again."

Before he got on his horse, he shook hands with us kids.

"No hard feelings," he said. "You had your hearts in the right place. Just be sure you look a little harder next time. Get your facts straight first."

He swung into his saddle, waved goodbye, and said he'd see us soon.

"Well, we're nowhere nearer finding the poacher than we were before," Carlos said as he watched Ben ride off.

"And I don't want you kids sticking your noses into this thing," Don said. "You need to mind your own business."

"Right," we all said.

But my brain already started coming up with ideas about how to try to help find the poacher. I felt so bad about being wrong about Ben that I couldn't stop myself. But how could we look for the poacher and stay out of trouble? I had to talk to Will and Allie.

EIGHTEEN

Return to Gooseberry Cabin

I asked Will and Allie to go with me to the campground so we could talk without anyone listening to us.

"Jessie, you're nuts," Allie said as we sat at one of the picnic tables. "Your parents will shoot you if they find out you're still hunting this poacher."

"And my dad'll kill me, too," Will said.

"I know," I said, "and I don't mean we should go running all over the place like Sherlock Holmes, snooping around with huge magnifying glasses. I just mean we probably know the poacher and can maybe figure out who it is if we just think hard enough. Then we can tell Warden Carlos and your dad, Will, and they can make an arrest. Wouldn't it be cool to say we helped catch him?"

"I dunno," Allie said. "My folks want me to come home in a couple days. If we screw this up, Will's dad may get mad and send us both home right now. Maybe we should just chill for a while."

We tossed stones at a stump to see who could hit it the most. Not exactly thrilling entertainment, but all of us felt low after learning that Ben wasn't the poacher. When we got bored throwing stones we watched Oriole and Casey frantically dig under a log. They came up with dirty brown noses and paws and a recently buried bone from someone's dinner, which Casey brought to Will and dropped in his lap.

"Geez," I said. "Someone buried a bone right in the campground so they didn't have to take it out? Talk about lazy. Looks like there are caches everywhere for Ben to clean up."

We sat quietly for a few minutes before hearing voices drifting up from the Big River Trail across the campground from our table.

"Finally. I thought we'd never get here," a female voice said.

The voice sounded familiar. I stood up to get a better look. Four backpackers walked single file into view. Coyote and his group had returned. They looked tired and filthy dirty.

"Boy, am I glad to see this campground," Emma said as she plunked down on a picnic table bench. "I don't think I could walk another step."

"Me either," Steve said, throwing his backpack on the wooden table. "That was a long haul."

"Maybe so," Tracy said, "but you did great, Steve. Must be you're getting stronger after backpacking for so long."

"I sure hope it's all worth it," Steve said.

Coyote swung his backpack off his shoulders and onto the table. "It'll be worth it, all right—if the boss is happy, that is." He looked up, jerking his head as if startled. "Oh. Looks like we've got company."

The conversation died as Will, Allie, and I jumped up from our table and ran to meet them.

"Hey, you guys," I said. "How'd the rest of your trip up Clack Creek go?"

Emma winced and rubbed her neck. "Not bad if you don't mind a death march. Coyote likes to push us hard."

"No pain, no gain," Coyote said, although he seemed relieved to have reached the campground, too. He actually smiled, something I didn't ever remember seeing him do.

"How long you going to be around?" Will asked. "Allie and I have to go home soon. We'd like to say goodbye first."

Tracy dusted off her long skirt and kicked the table leg to get rid of a dirt clod on the bottom of her hiking boots. "We're headed out for Scott Lake tomorrow for a day or two, so we probably won't see you again. You kids were great, though. And I love your dogs."

Oriole and Casey had already sidled up to Tracy and were sniffing her skirt and boots all over.

"Sorry they're so nosy," I said. "You must have great smells on you."

"We haven't had a bath in a while, so they probably smell food we've eaten and who knows what from the trails we've hiked. You know, lots of animals pass by and all. They probably smell them, too."

Coyote dug into his pack. "Well, we'd better get busy setting up camp. Gotta get up early and get moving if we want to make a full day of it. Maybe we'll see you around."

We said our goodbyes and headed back to my house. It was getting close to dinnertime.

We sat on the porch swing later that night while Mom and Jed played cards in the living room and Dad met with Charlie and Pete. The big thing we tried to figure out was why the four backpackers kept coming back to Schafer when they planned to spend the entire summer in the wilderness. There were too many other neat places to visit. Why return to some place they'd already seen?

"You don't suppose they're the poachers," I said. "They've been around a lot. And Ben and Lost kept seeing them."

"Yeah, but we don't know if they went near Scott Lake where the deer was killed," Allie said. "Anyway, I hope it's not them. I like them. All but Coyote, that is."

Our thought process hadn't gotten too far when Dad showed up. He stood against a log pillar on the porch, facing us with his arms and legs crossed.

"Don and Carlos want to visit the trail crew at Gooseberry and take a look up Clack Creek," he said. "They're leaving tomorrow. Will, your dad wants to take Casey with them as law dog. Pete's going as far as Gooseberry so he can take grain to the cabin and start bringing out some of the trail crew's stuff. I thought maybe you three would like to go along."

"Aw, Dad," I said. "We just got back from there not long ago. Can't we go somewhere else?"

Dad put up a hand to stop me. "I know you were there not long ago, but you seemed to like it well enough. And you could keep Pete company on the trip and give him a hand if he needs one."

I felt deflated. On the one hand, Dad could have been trying to make the visit with Will and Allie fun for us by giving us another trip to Gooseberry, but it didn't sound that way. It seemed more like he didn't trust us to be alone, like he thought we'd go off hunting the poacher by ourselves or something. And I love Pete but I didn't want him to be our babysitter. I didn't think we had a choice, though, so we each packed a bag for the trip.

Gooseberry Cabin stood against the mountains and the Middle Fork River. It looked so warm and inviting that I left my gloomy mood behind. The cabin appeared empty from the outside, but inside it was jam packed. The crew had laid out their sleeping bags on the two sets of bunk beds and hung their clothes on the ends. Shovels, saws, and pulaskis leaned up against the wall by the door, along with extra work gloves. Sandals sat neatly under beds.

Pete set up a tent outside for Carlos and him, and Don put up his and Will's tent. Allie and I pitched ours between the other two. We inflated our mattresses and sprawled out on our sleeping bags.

I turned on my side to face Allie and rested my head on my hand. "Where do you think Lost is? I expected to see his tent here. Wasn't he supposed to be visiting Cody?"

"Who knows? He's probably off on some other great adventure. Maybe he'll show up before we leave."

We had left the door to the small dome tent open. Oriole burst in, followed by Casey. Oriole walked behind Allie and stood next to my head. Her tail wagged wildly, and she panted with a happy look on her face as she glanced back at Casey. She practically pranced between Allie and me, almost stepping on my leg. Casey followed behind her. She stopped and looked back at Casey again. Then both dogs left the tent as quickly as they'd entered.

Allie and I stared at each other in amazement.

"I swear Oriole was bringing Casey by so he could see her tent," I said.

"I know. It was as if she were saying 'Look, Casey. This is where I'm staying tonight. Pretty cool, huh?' Those dogs are like people. It's scary."

We laughed and got up, zipping the tent on our way out.

Before we left Schafer, Dad had told us the trail crew would probably be working only a mile or so from the cabin. Although late in the afternoon, Pete planned to visit them, so we tagged along.

When Oriole and Casey began barking, first warily and then excitedly, we knew we'd found the trail crew. They dropped their shovels and other tools when they saw us and took a break. Celie asked what was happening at Schafer Meadows, Mandy wanted to hear all about our adventures, and Cody asked if Lost had made it back to Schafer.

"We haven't seen him since we were here last," Allie said. "When did he leave?"

Cody shrugged. "He's been gone a few days now. Said he was going straight back to Schafer and would hang out there until we got back from this work project. Unbelievable. Guess my crazy friend got lost again."

Pete sat across the trail from Celie. "How'd the Bowl Creek project go?"

"Really well. It's pretty much done, so we feel good about going back to Schafer."

While Cody and Mandy threw sticks for Oriole and Casey, the crew told Pete what things of theirs he needed to pack out the next day. Then we left the crew and returned to Gooseberry Cabin.

At the cabin, a large heavy backpack leaned against the building. We walked inside and found Lost sitting at the table with Don and Warden Carlos.

Don hugged Will and said hello to all of us. Carlos and Lost shook our hands absentmindedly, as if they'd been deep into a conversation and wanted to return to it. We sat quietly at the table so they could continue.

Don looked bewildered. "Tell us again how you ended up back here? Didn't you say you were going back to Schafer Meadows?"

Lost turned red and looked away. "That was the plan. I left a couple days ago intending to meet Cody back at the ranger station. The crew left to work on their trail project. I packed up my tent and my backpack, sat on the porch for a cold breakfast of granola bars and jerky, and left. Must've turned the wrong way on the trail, because I walked and walked and never got to Schafer."

"Didn't you realize things didn't look familiar?" I asked.

"Well, sure. After a while, that is. At first I walked through the trees, so I couldn't see out much, couldn't make out any familiar mountains or landmarks. Sometimes it all looks the same, you know, when you're surrounded by a wall of trees. After a while I realized I'd walked up Bowl Creek, because I recognized some of the trail crew's work. I decided to keep walking and find Cody to get directions."

Lost shook his head. "I never saw the crew, though. They must have taken a break somewhere off the trail or something, so I kept going. Then I really got lost. When I first left Gooseberry, I had taken a right turn to get up Bowl Creek, so every time I came to a trail junction, I made a right turn, hoping to make a circle. I figured eventually I'd end up either at Schafer or back at Gooseberry."

Pete laid out a map. He followed along with his finger trying to see where Lost had hiked. Don and Carlos looked over his shoulder. "So what did you see—lots of trees? Openings? Cliffs?" Don asked.

Lost smiled. "That's the best part. There was some incredible country. I got up really high and wound up on top of a mountain overlooking all this unbelievable scenery."

"Was the mountaintop forested or bare?" Pete asked.

"Mostly open. Seemed like I could see forever. Another trail took off from there but went downhill fast. I followed it a little. It had lots of switchbacks. It also went left so I went back up and took the other way—to the right."

Pete followed a line with his finger. A bunch of tight squiggly lines went off to the left.

"Switchback Pass," Pete said. He let his finger roam to the right. "Then what?"

"I ended up at the lake where I met those people earlier who had the hurt dog. It wasn't much farther once I'd gotten onto the trail that went right."

"Dean Lake," Don said. "So you decided to go back to Gooseberry from there?"

"By then I'd been out a couple days. I was running out of food. I'd left most of it with Cody because he likes my jerky so well. Normally I don't leave any food anywhere, because if I get lost I want to have enough to eat until I can find my way out. But I was really confident this time that I could make it to Schafer. Guess I should have taken my own advice and not left any food behind for Cody. But back to your question—I knew for sure I could make it back to Gooseberry from there. At least it was my best shot."

"Did you run into anyone else while you were out?" Don asked.

"Yeah. There was a guy riding alone pulling a mule and later a group of backpackers. They all said I was on the trail to Gooseberry."

Don stood up. "Guess you're pretty hungry after your ordeal."

"More like ravenous," Lost said. "Do you mind if I find my food? Cody probably left it here somewhere."

Lost got up and walked to a sack hanging from a nail on the wall. He pulled it down and stuck his nose inside. A big smile appeared on his face. "My good friend Cody didn't touch a morsel. Looks like I'll have a feast tonight. You're free to join me if you'd like."

"Thanks," Pete said, "but we came with more than we can eat."

Lost took the bag outside. Don and Carlos grinned and shook their heads.

"Let's talk with him later—after he's had something to eat," Carlos said. "Maybe he'll remember something else."

The trail crew would arrive soon, so we decided to fix dinner for them. I'm not much of a cook, so Will and Allie prepared macaroni and cheese while I chopped veggies. Carlos and Don sat at the table, poring over a map and discussing their trip up Clack Creek.

After dinner, we kids went to the river and sat on the bank while Oriole and Casey swam.

"What Lost said matches Ben's story," I said. "Remember Ben said he was up Clack Creek and saw four backpackers and a guy who looked lost?"

"Yeah," Will said. "Looks like Lost's story holds up."

"Good," Allie said. "I really like him, but it still doesn't mean he's not the poacher."

"I think we can rule him out," I said, tossing a stick to Oriole.

"Why do you say that?" Allie asked.

"Well, first of all, I think he really got lost. If he poached something, why would he come back here? Don't you think he'd take whatever he had poached and leave? He had no reason to come back."

I stared at the mountains. "And another thing—there's no way he would have shown up here starving. I don't think he'd have left his food."

Allie agreed. "Especially if he poached it in the first place."

"And don't forget he agreed to go back with us to Schafer tomorrow. I don't think a poacher would do that. He'd probably want to stay as far away from us as possible."

"You're right," Allie said. "I feel much better. I'm ready for a snack."

"Me, too," Will and I said together.

We jumped up and turned toward Gooseberry Cabin.

"Last one there has to serve the other two," Allie said, and she was off. Oriole and Casey raced ahead of her, while Will and I trailed behind.

NINETEEN

Hard Thinking

We returned to Schafer Meadows early the next afternoon with Pete and Lost while Don, Carlos, and Casey went up Clack Creek. Lost left us at the campground, saying he wanted to set up camp. I noticed the backpackers had already left. We unloaded our gear and helped Pete put the crew's belongings in the basement of the cookhouse for them to retrieve when they got back to Schafer. We took our own things to my house and dropped them on the porch.

We sat on the swing and thought about the poacher, trying to put the pieces together.

"Maybe it's someone we haven't seen," Allie said. "Someone lurking in the wilderness, laughing behind our backs."

Will shrugged. "I don't know. It's not like there are tons of people out there. I think we'd have seen them."

I scratched Oriole behind her ears. "I keep going back to Coyote and the other backpackers. They just don't make sense to me. They have all this country to explore and keep coming back here. Why?"

Will started the swing moving with his foot. "You know, sometimes people think they're going to do these huge trips into the wilderness but when they actually get here, they get scared."

Allie pushed the swing with her foot, too. "Yeah, I know what you mean. They think they're macho mountain men—or women," she added. "But when they actually get into the wilderness where they're on their own, they freak out. Getting around isn't as easy as it looks."

Will nodded. "So they find some place where there are lots of people and they hang out. Like here at Schafer, where someone's always around, or at Gooseberry Cabin. Maybe they knew the trail crew would be working from there."

"I see what you guys mean," I said. "You're saying they want to be tough but can't hack it, so they hang out near other people where they think it's safe and they won't appear scared."

I thought about that for a moment. "I don't think so. Not with them, anyway. Coyote doesn't look afraid of anything. And don't forget that he and Tracy went out together on business and left Steve and Emma at the campground while Steve's foot healed. I don't think they'd have left them behind unless they all felt okay about being split up. And don't forget, Steve had never been in the wilderness before. If he'd been that scared I don't think he'd have stayed here, no matter how much his foot hurt."

"So what are you thinking, Jessie?" Will asked.

"Just that maybe we should look harder at them as suspects, see if they fit."

"And then what?"

"And then if we find anything, we tell my dad or your dad and Carlos when they get back from Clack Creek."

Allie leaned over the swing in my direction and pushed her glasses up on her nose. "I'll go along with it, but only if you promise not to do anything stupid."

She sat back. "And only if you promise we won't say anything to anyone unless we have solid evidence that Coyote and his friends are the poachers."

Although I was a little bothered that Allie would think I might do something stupid, I agreed. "That's what I think, too. This could be really cool, but we'd all be in deep trouble if we goofed up again. Everybody'd be mad at us."

We walked to the other side of the airstrip, talking all the way. Our walking got slower as our thinking got harder. By the time we reached the other side we barely strolled along. We thought so hard and talked so much that soon we'd gone the entire half mile to the end of the runway.

"Okay," Allie said. "So when the four backpackers arrived at the campground they said they'd been in the wilderness a couple of weeks."

"Right," Will said. "And they'd seen a tall rider on horseback with a big mule and some guy who seemed lost. That had to be Ben and Lost."

"And we know Coyote and Tracy left Emma at the campground with Steve so Steve's blisters could heal."

"Yeah," I said, "and Coyote and Tracy went to meet some guy in Kalispell for a business meeting and to buy new boots for Steve."

"Wonder what kind of business meeting," Allie said.

"Wonder where they got the money for the boots," Will said.

I watched Oriole stick her nose in a ground squirrel's hole. "Wonder where they got the money for their whole backpacking trip. If they're college students, how can they afford to take the whole summer off and not work?"

"I know, seems funny," Allie said. "But maybe they're rich."

"Could be," I said. "But they don't dress that way. And Steve sure didn't have on good hiking boots when they first got here. In fact, now that I think about it, he wore cheap hiking shoes—not even boots. If he had money, he could afford good boots."

We had reached the Big River Trail going west. Will stopped. "Hey. When they got to the campground the other day, Steve said something about hoping everything was worth it, and

Coyote said it would be if the boss was happy. Maybe they're working here."

"Doing what?" Allie asked.

"Maybe research, or some kind of survey. I don't know."

I grabbed both of them by the arm. "Or poaching!" I said. "I just remembered something weird from when we first met them at the campground. Remember they were eating dinner when we got there?"

"Yeah, so what?" Allie said.

"So they offered us some of their meat—*fresh* meat. It looked like steak or something to me. Where'd they get it?"

"Coulda brought it in with them," Will said.

"Not if they'd been in the wilderness for a couple weeks like they said. Meat goes bad pretty fast back here if it's not refrigerated."

"You're right," Allie said. "Maybe you've found some-thing worth talking about. Let's look in the cookhouse for your dad. Last one there has to fix a snack."

Oriole stood by looking expectantly while I made snacks in the cookhouse. Dad wasn't there, so Will and Allie went to look for him. A note from Charlie and Jim said they'd gone fishing, and Pete was off somewhere.

The door opened and closed. Allie and Will came in and sat at the table.

"No one's around," Allie said. "Your mom left a note at the house that she had gone with your dad while he and Pete check on an overturned raft somewhere. She said not to wait for them for dinner."

"Great," I said. "The timing couldn't be worse."

"Worse for what?" Jed said, coming through the door. He sat at the table with us. I looked at Will and Allie, who stared at their plates.

"Worse for what?" Jed repeated.

I set down my peanut butter crackers. "Look, Jed, if I tell you something, you gotta promise not to tell Mom and Dad. They're both mad at me and I want to make them believe in me again."

Jed grinned. "That depends. If you promise to let me in on everything, I promise not to tell—unless it's illegal or something."

"It's not illegal. It's just that it could get us into more trouble than we're already in—if we're wrong, that is."

"Are you back on this poaching thing again? I thought they told you to keep your noses out of it."

"Look, Jed, we think we know who did it, but there's no one here to talk to about it."

"Okay, so talk to me."

We told Jed all the reasons we had that pointed to Coyote and the other backpackers as the poachers. When we mentioned the fresh meat at dinner that first night, I could tell he was hooked.

"Mom and Dad aren't here to tell right now," Jed said. "And I heard Don on the radio saying he and Carlos wouldn't be back at Schafer until late this afternoon. No one else is around. So we need to get proof some other way."

"We?" I said. "Yo, bro! You mean you're in this with us?"

"I guess so."

I felt relief. "We have to hurry if we're going to get any real proof. We can't wait for Mom and Dad. There's a chance the backpackers may leave the wilderness soon, maybe even tomorrow."

Jed took off his black cowboy hat and leaned over the table, arms and fingers stretched wide. He smiled slyly. "Tell you what I think. You said the backpackers mentioned going to Scott Lake. If we saddle the horses and hurry, we can reach the lake in an hour or so. If the backpackers are there, we can pretend we came to go fishing and snoop around some. Then if something links them to the poaching, we can hurry back here and let someone know."

"Wait a minute," I said. "I've got a better idea. Before we leave for Scott Lake, let's do a little planning. If we're right and they are the poachers, this might give us a chance to let an adult know before the backpackers can leave."

I had their attention.

"Here's what I think we should do."

TWENTY

Exposed

I felt sure our plans were good enough to catch Coyote and his friends in the act if they turned out to be the poachers.

We rode to Scott Lake, giggling all the way, eager to get there and test our ideas. Our saddlebags were stuffed full of tools. Oriole raced ahead, seeming to be caught up in the excitement. We pushed our horses in a fast walk, hoping to get to the lake with plenty of time to snoop around.

Jed tied the horses off the trail a half mile from Scott Lake so no one would see them. If anyone heard them whinny, they would think we were just arriving. Thankfully the horses hadn't made a sound. Jed led us on foot the rest of the way to the lake. Full backpacks hid our tools.

Scott Lake was smooth as glass, calm and quiet. We looked around, trying to act casual in case anyone saw us, but no one seemed to be there. So far, so good. We hoped to check out the area before the backpackers came back—if they were there, that is. Two tents snuggled against the trees near the lake indicated they hadn't left yet. Jed walked up to the tents.

"Anyone there?" Jed called.

No one responded.

"Let's take a closer look around to see if they might be nearby," I said quietly. "They didn't leave anything outside their tents. Maybe they're fishing at the lake."

Oriole sniffed around the tents but didn't wag her tail as if anyone had been there recently. We checked out the nearby woods, the edge of the lake, and the trail where it started up toward Flotilla Lake. There was no sign of anyone. Walking

back to the tents, I tried to look casual, but I was sure someone
a hundred feet away could hear my heart pounding.

Suddenly Oriole took off running, nose to the ground.

"Hey! Where are you going?" I called.

She kept going, so I ran behind, hoping she wouldn't
alert the four backpackers. Oriole went deeper into the woods
behind the tents. When I saw what she had smelled, I ran back
to the edge of the woods and called to Jed, Will, and Allie,
quietly but forcefully.

"Hey, you guys! Come here!" I waved them forward.

They hurried to me. I took them back to where Oriole
sniffed around.

"Check it out," I said.

A huge lean-to made from a tan tarp was tied to some
trees and hidden behind dense shrubs about 300 feet from
the lake. It was well away from view unless someone like us
stumbled onto it. We had to bend down to look inside, because
the bushes hid the opening so well.

"Wow, look at that!" Allie said. "Great nose, Oriole!"

"If this belongs to the backpackers, there's no doubt
they're the poachers," Jed said, pushing his black hat higher on
his forehead to get a better look. "Look at all this stuff."

My heart pounded and I shook with rage as I looked at
the contents of the lean-to. Bows, arrows, saws, knives, nets,
snares, and ropes along with other tools lay stacked on the
ground.

I touched a snare that had what looked like black fur on
it. "These aren't things a normal backpacker brings into the
woods. They look like poacher's gear. This must be where they
stashed what they poached. They must have kept it here until
they could get it out without being seen."

Jed stood up. "Either that or they left the wilderness as
soon as they got whatever they were after so they wouldn't
get caught. You know, like the paws from the mother bear. All

this can't fit in their backpacks. Maybe they plan some more killing."

Allie shook her head. "Gee, I sure wish we hadn't found this stuff. I really liked those guys—all but Coyote, that is."

To make sure we had proof in case we had to leave in a hurry, I took photos of everything in the lean-to. I turned off the flash even though it was still light out. The darkness inside the lean-to might set it off. We didn't want to take a chance that the poachers might see it. Will whipped out his sketch pad and pencils from his backpack and started to draw.

"What are you doing?" I asked. "We don't have a lot of time."

Will continued sketching. "What happens if your pictures don't turn out because the lighting is bad? There won't be any proof of what things looked like in the tarp when we got here. This should help. I'm drawing as fast as I can. Shouldn't take too long."

Allie looked out of the lean-to. "Guess this proves someone's a poacher, but it still doesn't mean the backpackers are."

"You're right," I said. "We gotta be absolutely sure it's them. Somehow we've got to get more information. But how?"

Jed put down a rope from the pile of tools. "Let's just hang tight and see what happens."

Will finished his sketch just as Oriole stood and looked toward the lake.

"Shhhh, Oriole," I whispered. "Don't bark."

Will peeked around the bushes by the lean-to. "Sounds like someone's coming this way. We'd better get out of here—now!"

We hurried away from the lean-to, angling deeper into the woods toward some huge spruce and Douglas-fir trees with branches reaching to the ground. We lay hidden on the ground under the trees. Whoever was coming couldn't see us, but we could see them and had a good view of the lean-to, tents, and lake. I patted Oriole and asked her again not to bark. She stood with hackles up and ears alert but didn't make a sound. I made her lie down in case her yellow coat seemed out of place if someone looked our way. Her black parts might act as camouflage.

"Good dog," I whispered, hugging her. "You're the best."

A minute passed and it felt like I had held my breath the entire time. Soon four figures walked silently from the lake. They stood by the tents and looked around as if to make sure no one saw them. Then they hurried into the woods toward the lean-to. Tracy led the way, followed by Steve, Emma, and finally Coyote. The disgust I felt for them overpowered my anger. I couldn't wait to tell Dad, Don, and Carlos.

Coyote took a large skinning knife from his pack, ran his thumb over the blade, put it inside the lean-to, and bent over to inspect some of the equipment inside. "Let's hope no one finds this stuff. I think we did a good enough job of hiding it."

"Let's hope we hid the lean-to at Clack Creek as well as this one," Tracy said. "It was hard walking away when that trail crew was so near."

"Not to mention everyone else who went by, like that guy with the tall horse and mule and that stupid lost backpacker."

Emma laughed. "Go figure. We probably saw just about everybody in the wilderness."

Coyote picked up a bow. I tensed, wondering if he planned to use it. He set it down in another place, though. "Well, let's get back to camp and make dinner. If we get an early start tomorrow, we can get to the trailhead in plenty of time to meet The Boss and find out what he wants us to do next."

They turned away from the lean-to and returned to their camp at the lake.

I stood and looked carefully in their direction. "Guess we've got our poachers. We need to get our plan in place before it gets dark. Let's go!"

TWENTY-ONE

The Party

Jed ran farther into the woods beyond the trees hiding us before circling back to the trail and our horses. Part of our plan included having Jed ride Rocky as fast as he safely could back to Schafer Meadows to get Dad and Pete if we found solid proof that the four backpackers were the poachers. He was the fastest rider and could get there the quickest. He'd ask Dad to bring Warden Carlos and Don and Casey if they had returned from Clack Creek. If not, we knew Dad and Pete would come.

Meanwhile, Will, Allie, and I snuck back to the lean-to. I made Oriole lie down and stay quiet while we worked. We thought it might take a long time, but it was still light out when we finished. There was no need to cover our tracks—there was no bare ground, just low shrubs and grasses. But I was scared that one of the backpackers might come back to the lean-to before we finished and we'd have to abandon our plan to keep from getting caught and hurry back to Schafer. One of us kept watch the whole time. The backpackers looked like they might stay at their camp for the night. Good news.

When we finished working in the lean-to we lay under the spruce and fir trees that had given us cover earlier. The backpackers got up from their camp, and for a moment I feared they would head our way, but instead they built a campfire by the lake.

"Whew! I thought we were going to have to make a break for it," Allie whispered.

"Yeah, me, too," Will said. "I sure hope Jed's on his way back with help. That's the only part of your plan that might go wrong, Jessie. If he can't get your dad or anyone else to come, we're in deep trouble. Sure wish we had Casey with us."

Dusk came. A blood-red sun filled the sky as day deepened into night.

"Must be smoke in the air to make such a deep red," Will whispered. "Wonder if there's a fire somewhere."

"Let's hope not," I said. "We don't need any more trouble now. C'mon. It's dark enough to move. Let's go."

We tiptoed from our hiding place under the trees to the lean-to and crawled from there to the shelter of a large log, not far from their tents. I couldn't believe how good Oriole was. She walked so quietly I almost forgot she was there. It was like she'd pulled in her toenails. I almost laughed.

As we watched, a chilling fog rolled in from the lake, separating the backpackers and their campfire from us and our log. We had a hard time seeing them through the fog, which meant they couldn't see us well, either. But it would be easy to hear what they said.

Steve poked the fire with a sharp stick. It roared to life. Shadows like something from Halloween loomed over the tents. "I'm starting to relax now that we're finally getting out of here. One more hunt and we're home free." He snickered. "Can't say I didn't enjoy it, though."

Tracy pulled her skirt into her legs and sat next to Steve. "Yeah. I could tell you were getting into it when you shot that bald eagle right out of the sky. Too bad when we set up that lean-to at Clack Creek we couldn't get close enough to that bighorn sheep to kill it, too. It would have brought a good price. Its horns had nearly a full curl."

"That's okay," Coyote said. "We know where it is now and can go back for it. Don't worry—we'll get it."

Even through the fog Coyote looked so smug I could barely stand it. He leaned back in his camp chair, put his hands behind his head, and crossed his legs. "Yeah. We're getting pretty good at hunting. And it's so easy to get away with it. Let's try for one of those pretty white mountain goats when we go after the bighorn sheep. Might as well rack 'em up. I just wish we could be around to see those law enforcement guys chasing their tails trying to catch us."

Emma backed away from the fire as the smoke turned her way. "Yeah," she said, laughing. "They've been at least one step behind us the whole time."

Tracy laughed, too. "All you need is to be one step ahead of them. That hasn't been a problem."

Steve held his arm out like he had a rifle in it. He swung it toward the lake and pulled an imaginary trigger. "Boom! I almost hate having to leave tomorrow. But knowing we'll come back for the bighorn sheep and mountain goat will make it okay."

It took everything in my power to stay still. I was seething. I looked at Will and Allie and could tell they felt the same way. If Jed didn't get back soon, who knew what might happen?

The backpackers stopped talking and just sat. After fifteen minutes their fire died down and we watched their flashlights as they went into their tents.

We kept watching the tents from behind the log. I heard a zipper. A head popped out of one of the tents. A dark form crawled out, stood, and moved slowly in our direction.

"Duck!" Allie whispered.

We flattened ourselves behind the log, barely breathing. I heard footsteps softly moving toward us. Oriole's ears perked up. I placed my hand on her back to keep her quiet.

"What's the matter out there?" Steve called from his tent.

"Nothing," Coyote said. "Just thought I heard something. I'll be back in a minute."

A flashlight beam tore into the menacing night over our heads. It searched the ground about twenty feet on the other side of our log and then fanned out over the trees in the direction of the lean-to. Then everything went black.

I heard a match strike. It sounded like he was just a few feet from us. A yellow glow lit the area near us. Then it disappeared. I heard Coyote take a deep breath and exhale. The stench of cigarette smoke wafted to us. I almost gagged.

Finally, he left. I heard his tent zip up. We carefully looked over the log. All was dark and quiet. I lay my head on the log and exhaled.

Hardly making a sound, Allie whispered, "It's a good thing he came out for a smoke. If that zipper had been from his jeans and he was as near as he was to us, I might have screamed bloody murder and run away."

Will doubled over, holding his stomach. "Shut up! Don't make me laugh," he whispered into the log.

I had tears running down my cheeks from laughing. It was hard to keep quiet, but we had to. We settled down again to wait for help to arrive. It seemed like forever.

"Finally! Here they come," I whispered.

Hoofbeats pounded the ground and lights bobbed into view. A dark dog flashed past us.

Casey!

Relief flooded me as I saw Dad, Pete, Carlos, and Don riding hard toward us. I took off my headlamp and waved it back and forth to signal where we were.

I jumped up from our log and ran to them. Motioning for Warden Carlos to bend down toward me, I whispered in his ear. "Don't worry about them having weapons—it's okay. We made it safe for all of us. If they try to use any, let them try. Trust me."

Will, Allie, and I left the log, ran past the tents and lean-to, and hid once more under the trees deep in the woods. Oriole raced with us.

The backpackers stumbled out of their tents. They saw the horses headed their way. Coyote flipped on a large flashlight as he ran toward the lean-to. "C'mon, you guys," he hollered. "Looks like trouble. We gotta get to those weapons."

We kids inched closer. Earlier, while the backpackers sat at the lake around their campfire, we decorated the lean-to with streamers that we brought in our saddlebags. They were left over from the Fourth of July party at Schafer. A hand-printed sign Will had made hung on the outside of the lean-to saying, "Welcome to the party!"

The three of us stayed hidden with Oriole under the trees. Coyote's flashlight lit up the lean-to, giving us a great view of the action. We held our hands over our mouth to keep from laughing out loud.

Coyote entered the lean-to. His head whipped back and his shoulders jerked.

"What? Where's—?"

Will, Allie, and I nearly burst with laughter.

Coyote came back outside carrying four bows and four quivers. For once, he looked speechless. He stared at Will's "welcome" sign, not seeming to understand what it was.

Carlos and Dad reached the lean-to, dismounting on the run. Carlos had his hand on his holster.

"Game warden," he said, showing them his badge. "Don't do anything stupid."

Coyote's face changed from shock to a sneer, and he got his voice back. He stood up straight, held tight to the bows and quivers, nodded toward the lean-to, and looked Warden Carlos in the eye. "What do you mean, don't do anything stupid? We're just having a party. See?"

Pete and Don moved next to Dad and Carlos. Casey stood ready for action.

Don stepped toward the backpackers. "Move away from the lean-to. Slowly."

"Sure," Coyote said, looking at his three friends. He grinned. "Sure. We'll do that." He tossed bows and quivers to the other three. They stood there as if ready to defend whatever was in the lean-to.

Coyote exploded into a run. The others did the same, going in different directions.

"Grab an arrow," Coyote hollered.

All four reached into their quivers. I peered through tree branches to see the looks on their faces. If it had been daylight, they could have caught flies in their open mouths.

They stared at their hands. Instead of an arrow with a deadly point, each held a toy arrow with a round rubber end, the kind you wet with your tongue to make it stick to the wall and it goes "thock!" when you pull it off. Daisies and thistles hung off of them—Allie's contribution. Will and I gave her a silent "high five."

When Coyote tossed the other backpackers their bows and quivers, they didn't look at them. They didn't know we had replaced the real arrows with toy ones. The arrows came from a set some little kid left behind in the campground at Schafer. Never thought they'd come in handy back then.

Steve looked at the toy arrow in his hand. "What did you do with our stuff? We've been robbed!"

That one really drew soft giggles from us kids. I buried my head in Oriole's neck and hugged her hard, partly because this was so much fun, but also to keep her—and me—quiet. Oriole stared ahead.

Warden Carlos had evidently taken me at my word that the poachers couldn't use their weapons. None of our rescuers had moved the whole time. I couldn't wait to hear what the poachers had to say about why they ran with fake weapons.

Don and Casey came up behind the group. Casey stood ready for action. Don looked past the backpackers. "What's in the lean-to?"

"Not a thing," Coyote said. He bowed to the men. "Come look for yourselves."

Don stayed back with Casey.

Dad, Pete, and Carlos entered the lean-to.

Pete exited first. "He's right. It's empty."

Dad came out. He buried one hand in his hair and placed the other on his hip. He looked down at the ground. After what seemed like an eternity, he looked at Warden Carlos and said, "I don't understand. Jed was so sure—"

I felt bad. I wanted to run to Dad and tell him it was okay, that Jed was right. But we had to let things play out—let the poachers trip themselves up. I kept quiet.

Coyote must be a fast thinker, because he came up with a line that sounded so good I didn't know how anyone could not believe him.

"Don't feel too bad," he said to Dad. "Other people have seen us and didn't understand what we were doing, either."

He stared at the other backpackers as if to make sure they didn't say anything.

"You see," he continued, "we love games. Paintball's our favorite, but it's not something we thought would be a good thing to play in the wilderness. You know, leaving these little round balls and splotches of paint all over the place. It's just not cool. So we're working on a game like paintball but with bows instead of guns. And instead of real arrows, we thought we could put paint on the rubber ends of these toy ones. It wouldn't be as dangerous."

Emma butted in. "Yeah, that's right. And it wouldn't harm the environment. It's gonna be a great game when we get all the kinks worked out of it."

Tracy held up one of her rubber arrows. "Ought to be able to make a bunch of money someday."

"So why the lean-to?" Dad asked.

Tracy moved to it, grabbing a pole that held up one end. "That's headquarters. It's where we keep our gear until we want to play."

Dad nodded and looked at Steve. "And what's your name, son? Steve, is it? What'd you mean when you asked where your stuff was? You said you'd been robbed."

Steve shrugged. "Oh, that. I—I thought someone had taken our gear. I forgot we packed it up to go out tomorrow. Everything but the bows and quivers, that is."

Coyote got that smug look on his face again. "See? There's nothing to worry about. Sorry you came all the way out here for nothing."

I couldn't stand it anymore. I stood up and left the safety of our tree hideout.

"Sorry, Dad, but you need to know this. You didn't come here for nothing."

Will and Allie stood, too.

Oriole ran to Casey, her tail wagging wildly. Casey stayed on guard. Oriole took her cue from him. Neither dog moved a muscle.

Carlos crouched down and pointed to something small leaning against one pole of the lean-to. "What's that?"

Allie flashed her headlamp on the object. A teddy bear sat leaning against the tarp. One back leg was caught in the angry-looking teeth of a leg trap.

Allie practically growled in anger as she said, "You guys killed a mother bear with a cub. Don't you even care?"

Tracy sprang the trap, freeing the teddy bear's paw. "Real funny. Ha-ha. But you don't have any proof."

I turned to Dad. "We have plenty of proof," I said. "You won't find anything there because we moved it."

Will bent down on one knee and hugged Casey, who still stood on guard. "Jessie's right, Dad. The 'stuff' that Steve meant when he said they'd been robbed? There's plenty of it. And don't worry. It's in a safe place. They'd've never found it."

"Take me to it," Carlos said.

We took the game warden deeper into the woods to a large rock next to a dense patch of three-foot alder bushes. We had to wade through the waist-deep shrubs to reach the rock. Neatly stacked were the poaching tools from the lean-to, including the arrows that we'd removed from the poachers' quivers.

In my headlamp I caught a glimpse of Tracy's face. It was as red as her scarlet skirt.

"Dad!" I said. "We did it! We found the poachers."

Coyote whipped his head in my direction, a look of terror on his face. He took off running toward the lake. The other three ran with him. Coyote tripped and fell flat on his face. The others couldn't stop, ran into him, and fell on him like a stack of dominoes.

Coyote had tripped over a rope we'd stretched between two trees low to the ground in case the backpackers tried to escape.

"Great job," I said to Will and Allie. "It worked."

The poachers got up to run again. At Don's command, Casey ran toward them, growling and snarling. Oriole did, too.

Steve, Tracy, and Emma stopped dead in their tracks, but Coyote took off. Casey and Oriole had no trouble keeping up with him. Coyote fell to the ground. The dogs circled him, teeth bared.

I hollered, "See what it's like to be stalked like an animal? Scary, isn't it?"

Coyote kept his eyes on the dogs. "Shut up, you little worm."

"Guess you don't like it so well yourself," I called out. "Try to get up. Try to get away. See how long you last. Those dogs'll have you for dinner."

"That's enough, Casey, Oriole," Don said. "We'll take it from here."

Oriole and Casey backed off. Carlos and Don walked up to the poachers, who stood quietly, wide-eyed with fear. Even Coyote looked scared. Carlos handcuffed Coyote.

"You four have some explaining to do," he said.

Pete cuffed Tracy, and Don put handcuffs on both Steve and Emma.

Emma began to sob. "I knew it was too good to be true. We should have never thought we could get away with this."

Dad reached me and gave me a huge hug, like he'd never let go. Then he held me back at arm's length.

"What were you thinking, Jessie?" he said. "You could have gotten yourselves into serious trouble."

"We tried really hard not to, because I knew you'd worry. But am I ever glad to see you." I returned his hug.

Carlos took out the key to his handcuffs. He grabbed Coyote and uncuffed him. "We're going to turn you loose for now. I don't want any of you hurt getting out of here. But don't even think of trying to leave without me. I'll officially arrest you when we get to the trailhead at Morrison later."

He turned the poachers toward the trail back to Schafer Meadows. "You'll have plenty of time to talk when we get to the ranger station. Let's go."

Our flashlights lit the darkness. I rode Red toward Schafer Meadows, away from where we had found the dead deer. I looked down on the poachers who walked with drooping heads single file in front the law officers and us.

TWENTY-TWO

Explanations

What luck! Because it was night and too late to walk out of the wilderness, Carlos decided to keep the four poachers at Schafer Meadows until morning. Carlos was really mad. He made them carry their own backpacks with their personal gear to Schafer. Lucky for them they had too much poaching gear to haul out on their backs. Pete and Don would have to bring it out as evidence the next day.

We got back to Schafer really late. Mom met us at the cookhouse, and I could see worry fall away from her face when she realized we were all right. I ran and hugged her. She stroked my hair and patted Oriole. Charlie, Jed, and Jim had stayed up with her, keeping coffee and hot water going. They looked relieved to see us, too.

"We'll talk about this later, Jessie," Mom said. "We'll have lots to discuss. But Warden Carlos wants to talk with you first about the poachers."

As we sat around the kitchen table in the cookhouse, I told Carlos about seeing a tarp up Clack Creek when Jim took us kids flying. It looked like the lean-to at Scott Lake where the poachers stored their gear. Carlos asked Coyote's group about the other tarp. The four poachers just stared down at their hands.

"Look," Carlos said. "We'll find it if it's there. I can cut you a little slack, but only if you help me."

No one said anything for a long time. I could hear everyone breathing around the table.

Finally, Emma squirmed in her seat. "Look. I don't want to get into any more trouble."

Coyote folded his arms and glared at Emma.

She stared pleadingly at her other two friends and said, "There is another lean-to up Clack Creek. It has traps, snares, and other poaching tools like those stashed at Scott Lake."

Steve and Tracy relaxed as if they felt they could talk now, too. Coyote glared at them.

Steve told Carlos where they'd hidden the Clack Creek lean-to. I felt sorry for Don and Pete. Not only did they have to bring out the stuff from Scott Lake but they'd have to go there, take pictures of everything, and haul it out, too. These poachers really made a lot more work for everyone.

Don opened his hands wide. "I've got one big question for you four," he said. "Why? Why'd you do it?"

Coyote clenched his jaw and glared at him. "None of your business."

"Oh, just drop it, Coyote!" Tracy said. She started to cry. "Look. We never meant for things to go this far. We wanted to have fun, live off the land, spend a great time in the wilderness just as good friends."

"Yeah," Emma said. "But when Tracy says living off the land, she didn't mean killing animals. We planned to pick berries and roots and stuff. We thought we had enough dried food to last us the summer, but we didn't."

Steve nodded in agreement. "At first we intended to use the lean-tos as shelters, places to store and dry plants, but we weren't very good at gathering stuff. We got hungry. We had brought guns with us for protection but never intended to shoot anything for food."

Emma wiped back a tear. "Yeah, but then a deer came by, and rather than leave the wilderness because we weren't 'real mountain men and women,' Coyote talked us into killing it. He said people do it all the time and no one would ever find out. He said if anyone heard us shoot our guns we could say we were doing target practice."

"Yeah," Steve said. "We were hungry and too dumb to tell Coyote we wouldn't kill something just to be able to stay in the wilderness a while longer. So we killed several deer. To keep from getting caught with a lot of meat, we took just what we wanted to eat and left the rest to rot."

I thought of the deer we found on the side of the trail to Scott Lake. I couldn't believe someone would illegally kill a beautiful animal just to stuff their bellies so they could stay in the wilderness for a few more days. What a waste! It made me sick.

Emma looked hard at Coyote. "But what we didn't know was that Coyote hoped all along we'd eventually have to poach something. We listened to Coyote and let him lead us into trouble by killing that first deer. Once that happened, there was no going back. He said we were accomplices and were as guilty as him."

Coyote looked at Emma like he was really mad, but Emma went on. "He had a contact on the outside he called 'The Boss' who said he'd buy hides, horns, antlers, claws, teeth—you name it—for big money. The Boss brought in a couple mule loads of poaching tools to Scott Lake and Clack Creek. He stashed them in the woods and told us how to find them. That's why we went to Clack Creek—to store those tools and hunt."

Tracy spread out her skirt. "Once we killed that first deer, it got easier from there. I guess I was partly afraid of Coyote and what he might do if I didn't go along with him, and partly excited about making easy money for college. When Coyote told us what The Boss would pay, we were all in. We killed several animals and began looking for those that might bring the most money."

Steve looked at us sheepishly. "All of you here took real good care of me when my shoes wrecked my feet. While Emma and I stayed at the campground waiting for the blisters on my

feet to heal, Coyote and Tracy took out the first of our goods.
Those two were the strongest and could carry the most out, so
Emma stayed with me. I felt bad knowing that I was abusing
your hospitality, but I didn't feel bad enough to let the money
go by. When Coyote and Tracy came back, I knew I wouldn't
stop."

Carlos sat back in his chair and stared at the ceiling. "So
tell us about the mother bear—the one you killed."

Emma sighed again. "We had decided to go up Schafer
Creek to hunt for animals. About a mile or so later we saw the
bear, not a hundred feet away. She came from the Dolly Varden
Trail and didn't see us until she had turned in our direction.

"Coyote had bought us backpacks that hide a bow. He had
stopped to rearrange his pack and had his bow and an arrow
out. He was getting them ready in case we came upon something when the bear saw us. She looked as startled and scared
as we were. Before she could turn to run, he shot her. She ran
back up the trail where she had come from, staggered into the
woods, and fell."

Coyote sneered and looked away.

Emma choked back a sob. "It wasn't until then that we
saw the cub coming down the trail after her. We're lucky the
mother ran away instead of straight toward us to protect her
cub. Honest—if I'd have known she had a cub, I'd have torn
Coyote's bow and arrow from his hands to stop him from killing her."

Tracy cried harder. "The bear died and the cub sat nearby
bawling while we sawed off the mother's paws. I never felt so
bad. But there was no way we could kill the cub, too. It was
innocent."

I couldn't stand it anymore. I stood up and jabbed my
finger in Tracy's direction.

"Innocent? Wasn't the mother innocent too? It didn't

bother you to cut off the mother's paws in front of her cub," I blurted out. "And you didn't feel bad about Coyote killing the bear in the first place and leaving it to rot. All you really cared about was the money."

I started crying, too. I pushed back my chair and ran out of the cookhouse. Oriole made it out the door before it slammed shut behind me. I sat on the bench next to the door, held Oriole tightly around her neck, and cried and cried. I thought I'd never stop.

TWENTY-THREE

Friends, A Gift, and Eggs to Order

The next morning dawned clear and sunny. My eyes felt puffy from crying so much the night before. Allie and Will sat on the porch swing of our house, waiting for me to go to breakfast. Casey lay on the grass.

"How you doin'?" Allie asked.

"Oh, I'm all right," I said. Oriole lay her head in my lap. Her wagging tail swept the porch. "How 'bout you?"

"I'm okay. I'm glad you let Tracy have it."

"Me, too," Will said. "She deserved it."

I threw a stick for Oriole, who bounded after it. "I'm just glad it's over. I'm glad they can't kill any more animals."

I felt better. "Let's go see what they plan to do with those four."

When we got to the cookhouse, Mom, Dad, and Jed sat at the table, just starting to eat. Oriole normally isn't allowed in the cookhouse during meals, but she snuck in. I made her lie down by the door.

"Pull up a stump," Dad said to us. "You might want to grab something to eat soon, Will. I think your dad wants to get you and Allie back home."

I felt my stomach drop.

"You mean Don's not going with Pete to get the evidence from the poachers?" I asked.

"Nope. Don has a lot of paperwork to do on this case now. But you kids might like to know that Don asked Spotted Bear to call Ben Morris this morning on the Forest Service radio. Ben will be back with his big horse and mule."

"Ben?" I said. "Did he forget a cache he made and wants to clean it up?"

"No. He agreed to come in as a volunteer this time. He's going with Pete to bring out the evidence you kids found at Scott Lake. I'm going up to Clack Creek. And Jessie, you and Jed are going with me."

Jed got a big smile on his face. "Cool! It's been a while since I've been there."

I felt differently. "Aw, Dad, we just got back from Gooseberry—again. Do I have to go?"

"You saw the tarp up Clack Creek where the poachers stashed the rest of their tools. You can help me find it. Besides, you and Jed and I need to have a long talk. Your mother and I aren't too pleased with you kids taking matters into your own hands to catch the poachers. You were specifically told to let Don and Warden Carlos handle things. Who knows what would have happened if we hadn't gotten there when we did."

I stared at my feet. "Sorry Dad, Mom. It was the last resort. We were afraid the poachers would get away. We really did try to let someone know, but nobody was around."

Mom sat next to me at the table. "That's no excuse. Don and Carlos are trained law enforcement officers. It was their job to catch them, not yours. If you had just let them handle it, they would have gotten the poachers sooner or later. What you did was irresponsible. You put everyone at risk."

Dad broke in. "Don and Carlos spent a long day riding back from Clack Creek, and because of you kids they had an even longer day. And your mother and I were worried sick. Think how you'd have felt if Oriole had done something as foolish and reckless as you did. Did it ever occur to you that she might have been hurt?"

The horror of what we'd done hit me hard when Dad said that. I never dreamed that my plan to catch the poachers would put any of us in danger, let alone so many other people. And

Oriole. She was my responsibility. I endangered her as well as everyone else.

Tears welled in my eyes, and I could barely whisper as I looked at Dad. "I'm sorry. I truly am."

Jed looked at his feet. "I'm sorry, too, Dad. It was partly my fault. I'm older and should have known better. It won't happen again."

Dad pushed his plate away. "You're not kidding it won't happen again. Warden Carlos wants to talk to you before he hikes the poachers out to Morrison and drives them to Kalispell."

"Well, good riddance," I said. I didn't want to see them again.

Carlos asked us to sit next to him. "Look, I'm glad the poachers were caught. I'm amazed that you were able to figure out who was killing these animals. But I need to explain a little about what you did last night that wasn't so good. I'm not here to scold, just to tell you how I see things. From a law enforcement point of view, it's too bad you moved things from the lean-to. It would have been better if they'd been left there."

"We know," Allie said, "but when we first got to Scott Lake and saw all the stuff there, we couldn't take a chance that the poachers would use it against us—or anyone else."

"Yeah," I said, pulling out my camera from my pants pocket. "I took pictures from within the lean-to before we moved everything, and Will has a great drawing. We hoped that would be good enough."

Will took his sketch pad out of his pack and showed the drawing to Carlos.

Carlos looked at Will's sketch. "This is good. If it matches up with Jessie's pictures, we can use both against the poachers in court if we have to."

Carlos nodded to Dad and Don. "The kids have all the evidence to prove that these four are the poachers. They did an excellent job." He looked at us kids. "Just don't do it again."

I was no longer hungry for the breakfast I had looked forward to eating. "Is this why Will and Allie have to leave now? Because of what we did?"

Mom passed around orange juice to us kids. "No, it's not. Don had promised Allie's parents that she'd be back home in the next day or so. But that doesn't let you off the hook. We'll talk more about this later."

Allie pushed her glasses up on her nose. "We're all sorry. We didn't mean to cause any trouble. My parents won't be happy, either. I hope we can still stay friends with Jessie and Jed."

"As far as we're concerned you can," Mom said. "And even though we're not happy with what you did, we're proud that you were clever enough to figure out who the poachers were. That took a lot of thinking."

"And at least we got to help solve a mystery before we had to leave," Allie said. "That was neat."

"Yeah," Will said. "Plus we got to become really good friends. That's even neater."

My heart swelled. I felt like I no longer needed to worry about Will and Allie leaving. They'd be back, and not just for a short visit. They'd be back as my friends.

"One more thing," Dad said. "Carlos got Coyote to tell him who 'The Boss' is. He plans to prosecute him for buying illegally taken game parts. Oh, and I almost forgot. Carlos called the Helena wildlife rehab center. They're sending some people to look for the orphaned bear cub to take to the center. That about wraps it up."

Charlie sat next to me and pushed a small wooden carving in my direction. "I finally finished this. It seems like the right time to give it to you. Hope you like it."

My eyes almost popped out of my head. "Oh, Charlie!" I said. "This is unbelievable!"

In my hands I held a life-like carving of Oriole. He had
found a piece of yellow wood with some kind of black knot in
it that he carved to look like Oriole's black ear, eye, and chest.
The little wooden dog stood as if ready for action.

"This should be in a museum," I said. "But it won't—it'll
be with me wherever I go. Oh, thank you, Charlie!" I hugged
him with all my might.

Charlie's gift and the fact that I had two new close friends
made me feel better than I'd felt in a long time.

"What's for breakfast?" I asked, suddenly starved again.

"Eggs to order," Mom said, smiling. "How'd you like
yours?"

I walked over to Oriole and knelt down, giving her a huge
hug. She licked my face and thumped her tail. "You know,"
I said, "I love eggs. I love omelets, quiche, frittatas, and just
plain eggs. I love 'em fried, scrambled, hard-boiled, and soft-
boiled. But you know how I love them best?"

I grinned.

"Poached!"

About the Author

Beth Hodder worked for the U.S. Forest Service for over 25 years, almost entirely with the Flathead National Forest in Montana. Part of that time her work took her to the Schafer Meadows Ranger Station in the Great Bear Wilderness, where her husband, Al Koss, was a wilderness ranger. Her first book, *The Ghost of Schafer Meadows,* won a 2008 Independent Publisher Book Award. A native of Ohio, she and her husband and dogs, Dusty and Scout, make their home in Montana.